My Loch Ness Journey

Look for More Terrorlands Books
by Marco Chu Kwan Ching

TERRORLAND

My Loch Ness Journey

MARCO CHU KWAN CHING

A
PEAR
PAPERBACK

ISBN: 978-0-6486552-3-7

First printing in 2019

PART 1

1

"Michael, we must retreat back to the shore before the storm hits!" Owen's voice came out muffled as if carried away by the wind.

The sky darkened.

Bolts of lightning cracked the inky sky.

Angry choppy waves echoed across the gigantic loch, rolling in and out.

Michael ignored his brother.

Although every cell in his body was screaming at him to turn back, he persisted.

"No. We must press on. There is no turning back now," Michael turned to Owen.

Continuous icy rain pattered on their face.

Heavier and heavier.

"Are you crazy! Are you risking our life for a mere legend?" Owen protested.

The wind rose again.

Tall foam waves towered over their helpless yellow boat.

The seagulls above their head were like tossed paper caught in the storm, struggling against the gale.

"It is no legend. It is right beneath the loch. I knew it." Michael insisted.

"Brother. I just want to go home. Please," Owen pleaded.

No matter how hard Owen tried, his stubborn brother turned a deaf ear to all sign of warnings.

Thunders cracked the ominous black clouds.

The wave grew mountainous that their boat was dwarfed, riding up and down like child's toy.

"Look out!"

Before Owen could react, Michael slipped on the wave soaked deck.

Crack!

"Ouch! I broke my ankle. I broke my ankle. Pain. Pain," Michael clenched his teeth.

Owen hurried to help his brother.

"Are...are you all right? Can you stand up?" Owen stammered.

Michael tried but the pain was unbearable.

"No. I am afraid I have to count on you now," Michael's expression turned grimace.

"But, I... I don't even know the way. What shall we do? What shall we do?" Owen panicked.

"You have to try!" Michael roared.

Lightning struck once more.

A mysterious huge shadow with a long neck flashed behind the brilliant shock of white in the graphite sky.

"Mi...Michael! Did...did you see that?"

"See what!"

"Dad, what did our Grandad see?" I pursued.

"Leon, he sees it is time for bed," Dad teased.

"But, Dad, I want to know what happens next. Otherwise, I will have to wait for a *looooooong* time," Leon implored.

"It is very late now. Mom is keeping a hawk-eye on you. You have an early flight tomorrow," Dad shook his head.

"Come on, I never see Grandad in my life. I want to know more about his stories. Dad, please."

Dad motioned to the cuckoo clock on the bedroom ceiling.

The little door slid in the clock opened. An eerie, cuckoo jumped out.

Cuckoo! Cuckoo!

It flapped its yellow feathers and squawked at least ten times before jumped back inside the clock.

"Stupid bird," I whispered, disappointed.

"Wilson, are you telling Leon all those wild stories again?"

A booming voice from nowhere made Dad and I startled.

When Dad and I turned around, we saw Mom crossed her arms, standing at the door wearing her pyjamas.

"Ummm... Actually, no," Dad choked.

"No more excuse," Mom snapped. "Leon, remember, you have a very early flight to catch."

She switched on the light.

The blinding light almost made me reach out for my sunglasses.

Great! I can't sleep now.

I squinted at Mom as she cautiously walked inside one step at a time as if there were landmines.

"Leon, your room is a mess. What is happening with you? Legos scattered everywhere on the floor. Empty Yakult bottles all over the table. How many times do I have to tell you to stop drinking so many of them? It is no good for you." Mom exclaimed.

"Ops." Dad swallowed hard and began to retreat.

"Mom, Yakult has beneficial bacteria," I disagreed.

"But, you are overdosing. And have you been listening to what I said? Look, I can still see your underwear from last week half left hanging on the cupboard. I remember I told you to put that in the laundry basket! Now, you make me wonder if you have even packed your luggage yet," Mom cried.

"Of course I have packed, Mom, of course. I am flying Scotland tomorrow, don't you remember? And I have been waiting for this for a *loooooong* time," I said.

"Good. By the way, Uncle Tony will be picking you up at the Glasgow airport tomorrow when you land," Mom continued.

"Uncle Tony?" I felt ecstatic.

Uncle Tony is absolutely amazing. He is adventurous,

charming and has a good sense of humour. I still recall a couple of years ago he brought Sam and I to go fishing by boat in the middle of Lough Currane. We waited till high tide at dusk. I still remember we stayed on the boat and watched the last orange-ray stretched far and wide, and then disappeared in the horizontal. I almost freaked out when Uncle Tony joked that we would stay on the boat till midnight. And we did! That night, Uncle Tony caught fifteen monster size king salmon under moonlight. They were delicious.

When I ask Uncle Tony why we stay up till midnight, he said the best time of the day to harvest salmon when it is dark. Salmon feed heavily during the middle of the night. During the daytime, they rest. Fullmoon is the best time to fish salmon at night.

A ringtone from Sam interrupted my thought.

When I look at my iPhone, I saw Sam's text.

"Dad said he will pick you up tomorrow at nine. Jesus, I can't wait to show you what we have captured on camera today."

3

The morning breeze of Scotland was chilling.

Here I am now, standing right inside Glasgow International Airport.

A nine-hour flight had delayed for almost an hour before it landed.

I wasted no time and headed straight to the baggage carousel.

The inky black mouth of the baggage carousel looked like that of an almighty worm.

As expected, my luggage took forever to come out.

I waited and waited, but there were still no signs of them.

Every time this happens, I always have a bad feeling I have lost my luggage.

Do you share the same thoughts?

I couldn't help to stop yawning the whole morning.

Even the old lady who sat at the aisle seat on the plane looked more refreshed than the nine years old me.

Well, the truth is I couldn't sleep on the plane last night. Not at all!

I was cornered in the window seat the whole time.

The old man next to me never stops sneezing.

The big fella in front of me violently reclined his seat, leaving me no room to move.

I twisted and turned in my seat all night. It was so cramped. At one point, it made me wonder if the plane seat had shrunk. I felt as if I am sentenced to prison for eight hours.

At long last, my two bags were finally vomited out of the mouth of the baggage carousel.

I swiftly lifted them up to the trolley, passed the custom, and headed straight to the international arrival.

"Hey, over here!"

A voice from nowhere drew my attention.

I glanced around the crowd in the international airport arrival gate. A casually dressed man in black sunglasses was holding up a sign labelled Mrs. Kwan. Behind him stood a family waving happily with smiling faces. A guy in brown leather jacket was more focusing on his Nintendo Switch than the wait.

"Hey Leon, over here!"

A Caribbean boy in a green T-shirt was waving in front of me. He had short afro faded hairstyle. He was skinny but very energetic. He couldn't stop smiling. His teeth looked exceptionally white and shiny in contrast to his chocolate skin.

He is my cousin Sam.

He is one year older than me.

One year wiser.

"Hey, Sam!" I waved back.

We hugged each other like long lost friends.

"Hey Leon, how have you been?"

"I am good. Finally, I am back again."

"Dad and I can't wait to see you. What took you so long?"

"You know…as usual…flight delay, and I never have the luxury to get my bags first."

"Don't worry, you have the luxury of time to join us to do some crazy stuff during the school holiday."

"I am sure I will enjoy. Where is Uncle Tony by the way?"

"Your flight was delayed. So, Dad just went to buy us some breakfast in case you are hungry."

"Good idea. The airline meal is terrible so I just skipped it."

"What else do you expect? A buffet or something?"

"Hey kid, we have hotcakes with butter and syrup, and sausage and egg McMuffin meal, and two hash browns."

A man from behind interrupted us. He is tall. He has a wavy short hairstyle with quaff at the front. He has an iconic horseshoe moustache.

"Uncle Tony!" I exclaimed.

"Leon, what did the time go?" Uncle Tony smiled.

He padded me on the back and hanged the meals to Sam and me.

"Yum. Dad, this is what I call a proper meal." Sam gave Uncle Tony a thumb up.

"By the way, what do you want to show me yesterday?" I asked.

"Here. Have a look." Sam shoved me some footages and photos.

"It is like Loch Ness."

"A few days ago, Dad was driving around the loch as we got to Urquhart Bay, just before the castle. I spotted something, something dark around three to four feet tall above the water surface."

I kept playing back to where Sam said.

But, everything happened in the split of a second, and I couldn't see it clearly.

"Well, it looks like a boat to me," I speculated.

"A boat doesn't lower itself into water and then disappeared," Sam said uneasily.

His eyes narrowed.

I focused on the footage.

Even I couldn't see it clearly, I clearly saw a turbulent wave pattern right after the dark shadow disappeared into the water.

What could that be?

Who would have guessed I was about to embark an unfathomable journey.

It is the winter school holidays in Scotland.

The gold and red colour of autumn gave way to the frost-blanketed street and snow-capped peaks. Some of the mountains have pyramidal shape. I was stunned by how massive the mountains were when I noticed a tiny village shadowed by it.

Occasionally, I saw helicopters patrolling the sky.

"Liathach & Beinn Alligin. It is best seen from high up on the peaks." Uncle Tony gazed at the rear mirror and signalled to change lane.

"Trust me. Don't go up there," Sam shook his head.

"Why not? It looks stunning." I narrowed my eyes.

"Dad and I once scrambled our way up onto the ridge. But, the descend was brutal. It was a thirsty finish for all of us." Sam recalled.

A moment later, we entered Edinburgh.

I sat back and peered outside the car window.

The car engine roared as we drifted up the driveway.

The stunning scenery of a loch sprawled out from our left. The undisturbed mirror image of pine forest on the other side of the loch was scenic. It almost reminded me of the Mirror Lakes in Fiordland National Park in New Zealand.

"Dad, where are we going today?" Sam asked impatiently.

"We are going to the famous National Museum of Scotland." Uncle Tony said.

"Dad, you work there! Aren't you bored already going there five days a week?" Sam teased.

"Wow, Uncle Tony, since when you worked in a museum?" I was amused.

"Since last year. Dad used to study rocks before," Sam giggled.

"No. Technically, not rock, but fossils. I am a paleontologist." Uncle Tony corrected.

"What is the difference between rock and fossils?" I asked.

"A rock is a natural solid aggregate of minerals. Fossils are the preserved remains or trace of animal, plants, and other organisms from the geological past." Uncle Tony explained and flashed me a smile.

"Dad is kind of weird. He can sit inside the garage looking at the same rock for hours until Mom complains. That is why he works in a museum now to share his passions with people about rocks," Sam whispered.

"Where is Aunty Belly by the way? I haven't seen her yet." I asked.

"Unfortunately, you won't be seeing her this time in your stay. She is in Africa busy chasing animals with her zoologist friends," Uncle Tony said.

"Or chased by animals," Sam murmured. "Oh wait, Dad, does that mean we will finally get the chance to go fishing salmon in Loch Ness?"

Uncle Tony didn't reply.

His broad smile in the rear-view mirror answered it all.

***

The streets in Edinburgh made me feel I travelled back in time in the nineteen century.

Victorian white sandstone tenements stretched all the way down the street.

A red, double-decker city sightseeing bus sent out a puff of black exhaust behind before it departs from the bus stop.

We waited until the traffic is clear before we crossed the road.

In front of us was the National Museum of Scotland.

Groups of tourists were already gathering below the poles for admission.

Facing one another on the piazza outside the front doors of the museum stood two statues.

They look so realistic that my weird imagination is telling me they will come alive at night.

"Dad, who are these people?" Sam asked.

"The one on the left is William Henry Playfair. He was a great designer of Edinburgh's classical landmarks. He designs the National Gallery of Scotland. The second statue is William Chambers who was the Lord Provost of Edinburgh in the mid-nineteenth century. He created the 1867 City Improvement Act to introduce a number of new streets. Can you read the street name on the sign over there?"

"Chamber Street," I replied.

"Yes. This street was named in his honour and remains as Chambers Street to this date."

We followed Uncle Tony up the stairs into the museum.

The main hall was flooded with people.

It had a cast-iron and plated-glass structure, which is a big contrast to the Venetian style.

According to Uncle Tony, there used to be two museums here. One is the modern museum of Scotland, and the neighbouring one is Royal Museum. They merged together to become the National Museum of Scotland.

My eyes darted left and right as we ventured in the Grand Gallery.

On the eastern end, the skeleton of a Tyrannosaurus Rex peered at us. Above it hung the taxidermy of a great while shark, a whale and a giant squid.

We marvelled over a spectacular array of animals on display.

A swimming Hippopotamus was stuffed and posed.

"Taxidermy makes me squeamish," Sam disguised.

"I guess the main theme of this part of the museum is about conservation of endangered species," I said.

"Even so, it is said trophy hunters can pay a lot of money for the right to kill a rhino and keep its horn," Uncle Tony said.

"Why is that so?" I asked curiously.

"Well, Rhino horn was reported to be selling more than that of gold or diamond by weight. People believe that rhino horn will cure everything from cancer to hangover." Uncle Tony shook his head.

We continued our way around the museum.

"Look, Dolly!" Sam exclaimed.

"Who is Dolly?" I frowned, looking around.

"Haha. Have a look. It is staring right at you," Uncle Tony pointed at a sheep.

"Do … do you mean Dolly the sheep?" I was amused.

I remember I read that Dolly is the first cloned mammal ever that sparked huge excitement to the public and the scientific world.

"Every time I stare into its eyes, I feel awe, maybe cloning is Noah's ark to the endangered animals outside," Uncle Tony whispered.

Just when we were about to move on, a man in a brown suit waved at us from a distance. He had red beard and small oval glasses. He looked like an Englishman.

"Dr. Tony, it has been a long time."

"Dr. Parker, same to you." Uncle Tony faked a smile.

"And who are these little ones?"

"This one is my son, Sam. And next to him is my nephew, Leon. Leon will be staying here during the winter school holiday."

"Very good. I am sure you will enjoy the Scottish landscape."

"So, Dr. Parker, what brought you to Scotland?"

"Well, just a plain visit. Let's say, for inspiration. The Natural History Museum always wants something more... something to capture public attention. And I can't get this inspiration anywhere else besides here." Dr. Parker tilted his glasses and evaded our glances.

"I hope this is the only reason," Uncle Tony said uneasily.

U ncle Tony had a holiday house in Loch Ness. Each school holiday, he will drove Sam and Aunty Belly there to escape the city life. Their favourite sport is fly fishing. Uncle Tony said Loch Ness never froze even in the very cold weather. And the native Atlantic salmon captured at this time of the year are monster size.

When did I learn fishing?

It all started three years ago when I first came to Scotland to visit Uncle Tony.

I was only eight.

I still remember Uncle Tony has a lot of patience teaching me fly-fishing.

But, I am just terrible at casting my fishing pole.

And my bait disappeared as soon as I lowered the pole into the water.

Sam said that I have no patience.

But, I don't really think so.

Believe me, fly fishing is not easy. Not at all.

The fish in Loch Ness is so clever that they just nibbled at my bait – one bite at a time.

Anyhow, I like fishing.

Fishing is just fun.

Even I do not catch as much as Sam.

"Leon, are you looking forward to your second at-tempt?" Uncle Tony teased.

"Sure I do." I winked.

"Leon, I got a boat driving license last week." Sam flashed his license.

"Wow, does that mean you can sail now?" I asked in disbelief.

"Sure. I can sail as far as I want," Sam said.

"Not too far. Remember how you fell into the loch last week when you insist to sail without me?" Uncle Tony warned.

"Dad, it was just an accident," Sam yawned.

"I only have one boat. I can't swim all the way to save you if you sail too far away from the shore. Not to men-tion the water is freezing cold," Uncle Tony complained.

"All right. All right," Sam said repeatedly.

The road to Loch Ness took about three hours.

It was such a bumpy ride that makes Sam and I drifted into sleep.

I had a dream.

I dreamt about Sam and I was in a small yellow wood-en boat. We were floating nowhere in the middle of a fogbound loch. Lost. We kept on paddling in the endless loch until we were hungry and exhausted. So, we decided to cast our fishing pole and hopefully caught a fish. But then, we heard strange noise in the fog. Sickening smell invaded our noses. Slowly, out of the fog, an enormous neck and head stuck out of the loch. Diving and surfac-ing, it approached us at full speed. The two of us were trashing our arms, screaming on top of our lungs.

"Leon, are you okay?"

Uncle Tony and Sam burst out in laughter.

"You almost hit my nose when you trash your arm in the air. What is wrong?" Sam asked.

"We arrived and were about to wake you up," Uncle Tony said.

"I… I just had a bad dream," I said in a low voice, feeling embarrassed.

"What did you dream about?" Sam asked.

"Oh, it is nothing. Maybe my dad kept telling all these spooky bedtime stories,"

"Oh well, you should relax. It is a school holiday. Besides, you haven't been to our new holiday house, haven't you?" Uncle Tony tested.

"Yes. I did," I said.

"Beats me, it no longer looks the same. So, are you signing up to catch monster size king salmon?" Uncle tony teased.

"Sure I do!" I exclaimed.

"Good man."

The three of us got off the car.

A gust of cold breeze enveloped us.

The sky was dyed in pink.

Orange gold stretched along the horizontal of the beautiful loch.

Here we were.

We arrived at Loch Ness.

"Magnificent, isn't it?" Uncle Tony exclaimed.

"Absolutely," I agreed.

"Each year, there is about one million people visit Loch Ness, in hope of spotting this legendary cryptid," Uncle Tony said.

"Do you mean the Nessie?"

"Yes. Over the years, there have been over one thousand recorded sighting of this monster." Uncle Tony continued. "Some explanations for Nessie sighting have included seals or overgrown eels. Others are just hoaxes that try to emulate the sighting of the monster."

"So, Uncle Tony, do you believe Loch Ness Monster actually exist?" I pursued.

"Sam does. I don't. Otherwise, I wouldn't go in the water," Uncle Tony padded Sam on the shoulder.

Sam giggled.

"What do you mean? Haven't you just captured the footage proofing the existence of the monster?" I frowned, darting back and forth at them, confused.

"Sam will show you when we get home."

"So, do you mean you make this up?" I realized.

"Hey guys, do you believe it? The footage has over one million views on Youtube." Sam was excited.

"People believe in what they want to believe. Loch Ness needs a monster. It worth half a million pounds to the Scottish economy."

***

I followed Uncle Tony inside his holiday house.

"Aunty Betty is away, so our home is a mess at the moment. But, please make yourself home. Your room is on the second level to your right."

I was stunned when Uncle Tony's holiday house came into view.

I don't recall Uncle Tony's holiday house to be like this luxury.

Not at all.

It looked as if it had been transformed from an old house into three stories, five bedrooms, modern living with a stroke of a magical wand. The bathroom and kitchen were stylish and spacious. Everything is tastefully decorated.

Uncle Tony must be rich.

"Since when did you renovate the house?"

"I didn't renovate. I sold the previous one and bought this. This one has a better view."

"Wow, Uncle Tony, you are incredible."

"I have just one rule in this house."

"What is it?"

"Stay out of the basement."

"Why is that?"

"It is a storeroom. Nuts and bolts lie scattering everywhere. It is all a mess inside right now. I have finished renovating everything except the basement. Now follow me. Your room is up there, on the second floor."

I followed Uncle Tony from behind as he settled my luggage. Then he led us to the balcony on the second floor.

As he opened the curtain, the last ray of the sun illuminated the scenic Loch Ness.

It was so incredible.

A folding balcony table was made of plywood. Next to it was a telescope mounted on a tripod facing the sky.

"Who wants to be my volunteer?" Uncle Tony offered.

"Me. Me. Me," Sam raced to raise his hands.

"You always have a chance. Why don't we let Leon try first since he is our guest," Uncle Tony said.

"Be my guest," Sam gave me a welcome gesture.

I peered through the telescope but everything was out

of focus.

Then Uncle Tony came forward and taught me how to adjust the knob to set the focal length.

"Better?"

"Much better," I gave him an okay signal. "The telescope was amazing. I can even see the detail of the rocks and gravel from across the loch."

"If you shift a bit to the right, you will see the famous Urquhart Castle. It is a landmark in Scotland that overlooks Loch Ness." Uncle Tony explained.

"Having fun? My turn. My turn." Sam asked impatiently.

"All right, guys. I will leave the two of you alone. I am going to take a shower. It was a long drive. Remember, don't fight over it. Take turns every ten minutes." Uncle Tony yawned and went downstairs.

"Here," I took a break after ten minutes and the smiling Sam took over.

I waited and waited.

"Sam, do you see anything interesting?

Sam didn't reply.

A moment later, his smiling face turned solemn.

"Sam?"

"Shhhh, quiet. I think I saw something," Sam whispered.

It makes me even more curious.

"Sam, can I please have a look?" I pleaded.

"Leon, you … you won't believe what I am looking at now."

"What is it? Tell me. Tell me."

Sam carefully shoved the telescope to me.

I cautiously rested my chin on the support and peered

through the lens.

But, all I saw was an undisturbed loch.

"Everything looks normal," I reported.

"No, focus. I saw something moving in the water," Sam declined.

"You always saw something in the water." Uncle Tony dried his hair with a towel as he made his way up the stairs.

"But, Dad, this time I really see it this time." Sam sounded disappointed.

"I think you are a bit too obsessed into this Nessie hoax." Uncle Tony shook his head. "If you believe in Nessie, why don't you start believing in witches too?"

"No. Witches only show up in American Horror Stories," Sam defended.

"Do you know in the 16th and 17th century, across Western Europe, many witch trials took place?" Uncle Tony asked.

"What does witch trials have to do with the Loch Ness Monster?" Sam was puzzled.

"The trials came about because, at the time, bad luck was attributed to supernatural causes. This mass-superstition proved to be extremely dangerous with thousands of innocent people dying as a result of the cases. Many of the trials had very low standard of evidence."

"So?" Sam shrugged his shoulder.

"You assume Nessie already exists and relates any water disturbance or strange object floating you see on Loch Ness is attributed to it. It is no different from those who attributed bad luck to supernatural causes, or those who believe in haunted houses and fortune-telling. It is pure peculiar follies and philosophical delusion."

Uncle Tony has a point.

The legend of the Loch Ness Monster has been around for a very long time.

Perhaps we believe in the Loch Ness Monster because we want it to exist, and not because it exists.

Perhaps there is no such thing as the Loch Ness Monster afterall.

Shades of grey dominated the sky.

Uncle Tony decided we go salmon fishing at dusk.

"Dawn or dusk after high tide is the optimal time to go fishing. It is best to avoid bright sunny times. Salmon prefers low lighting. That is why I like to pick overcast days like this."

We hopped inside Uncle Tony's yacht.

It had a spacious main deck with a master stateroom and two twin cabins on the lower deck.

Uncle Tony calls it the *Nirvana*.

"Baits, line, rod, rig." Uncle Tony counted as he passed the equipment to us.

"Hmm…. Dad, wait, what kind of bait do we need?" Sam scratched his head.

"Salmon roe,"

Salmon roe? Do salmon eat their own egg?

"But, we use them up last time, don't you remember?"

"I thought there are still some leftovers in the fridge."

"Na. All gone."

"Where did it go?"

"In my stomach."

"Dad, can we use cut bait instead?"

"Ya... I suppose. Cut bait will do."

I tried to help Uncle Tony and Sam to check if we have all fishing gears and accessories. To be honest with you, it seemed like the last century since I last fish. So, for me, everything is rusty. Do you believe it? I even spent the next thirty minutes trying to figure out how to thread the line through the eyelet of the fishing rod. As expected, I got it tangled.

"Sam, could you please give Leon a hand."

"Sure."

Nirvana lurched.

The yacht rocked hard left and right as we slammed against the wall.

"Whoa," I cried as I almost lost my balance.

"Sit down and grab the rail," Uncle Tony smiled and stepped on the accelerator.

The engine coughed, leaving patches of tiny bubbles in the churning water.

Nirvana sailed at the speed of light.

By the time I looked back, the Urquhart Castle became a tiny spot in our rear and then disappeared from sight.

I sat on the left bench in the main deck.

Behind me was a fisherman guide showing all type of fish in Loch Ness.

"All right, this should be the sweet spot," Uncle Tony announced.

"How do you know?" I asked.

"Hehe. I cheated a little bit. I bookmark the coordinates last time after following an expert. It is our secret night fishing location," Uncle Tony giggled.

Sam and I randomly grabbed a fishing rod each and

then attached a sinker with the bait.

We wasted no time and cast it as hard as we could.

WHOOSH!

As expected, we achieved only a short distance.

"Arghh, we can never do this right."

"Kids, watch," Uncle Tony said as he swept the rod forward to demonstrate a long-distance casting.

"Wow, how do you do that?"

"First, this rod is too heavy for you. You won't be able to load properly," Uncle Tony corrected.

"How about we use a much lighter line instead?" I suggested.

"Use too light of a rod is equally bad. It won't propel the bait at a long distance."

"So, how do we know which one is suitable to use?" Sam was confused.

"Pay attention to the weight rating of the rod and use lures that fall into the approved range." Uncle Tony explained and turned to my rod. "Another way to get more distance is to make sure your reel spool is full. Leon's one is only half full."

"What is a full spool?" I asked.

"A full spool means more line will come off each spool each turn and give you proportionately longer casts. Here, take these." Uncle Tony said as he repeated his cast. "Cast too hard is probably costing your distance because of the imbalance spool speed. Since the spool spins with a bait caster, the longer and smoother it spins, the longer the cast will be. Have a go."

Sam and I cast our rods again, but we only improved slightly.

"I know. It takes a lot of practice."

***

"WHOOSH!

We sat on each side of the bench, waiting forever for the rod to vibrate.

Dusk farewell us sooner than expected.

The last sunray dwindled behind the soft grey cloud.

The beautiful view of loch ness faded into blackness as the night has begun.

Uncle Tony switched on the submersible LED underwater fishing light.

The blue light was projected directly into the water and illuminated the water surface.

"Dad, Leon, look! Come and have a look! There is a big school of snappers here!" Sam exclaimed and motioned us to the light.

It looked spectacular.

"So many snappers, why don't they take a bite of our baits?" I complained.

"Perhaps your bait isn't there anymore," Uncle Tony laughed.

Gusts of howling wind whistled in our ears.

It was so chilly.

I am blessed to have a jumper on right now.

"Leon. Grab the net! Quick!" Sam shouted over the wind.

I quickly grabbed a landing net from behind and kneeled down beside Sam.

When we lowered it into the water, all the snappers scattered away.

"How disappointing!" I uttered a long sigh.

"Not quite," Uncle Tony disagreed as his rod began to shake and blend.

Crank Crank Crank

"We are getting a bite. We are getting a bite"

"Stay on the course!" Sam cried.

"It…it is heavy," Uncle Tony ground his teeth bitterly. His face was all red.

"Reel! Reel! Reel!"

"We got the colour! We got the colour!" I exclaimed.

"It is a big one,"

"Reel! Reel! Reel!"

I have never seen Uncle Tony's hand reeling this fast before.

It was like a machine.

Crank Crank Crank

The fishing rod continued to blend.

The fish must be *hugeeeeeeee.*

My heart was pounding fast.

I watched from behind Uncle Tony as he continued to battle the fish. I have never seen him like this before. The closest time I have seen him like that was when he caught a one hundred pound salmon a few years ago. But, that time, he had a friend with him. This time it is only us.

Water was splashing violently in the churning water.

The colour faded momentarily into the black water and resurfaced again.

"Sam, quick. Spear it! Spear it! QUICK!"

7

A jumbo size!

Sam silenced the monster with the strike of a spear.

Uncle Tony pulled the monster up, and onto *Nirvana's* deck.

The monster flipped and flipped until it finally bites the dust and passed away.

Everyone gave each other a high-five in triumph.

"Welcome on board," I mocked.

"We landed a big fish this time," Sam clapped.

"Guys. Good teamwork... look at that. It...it is probably the biggest Atlantic Salmon I have ever caught," Uncle Tony laughed breathlessly.

"How many pounds?" Sam asked, jiggling two fish in one hand.

Uncle Tony lifted the fish on a crane scale.

"One hundred pounds!" Uncle Tony was amused.

"How much can we sell for one pound?" I asked.

"The market is around sixteen bucks a pound. In order words, the fish just bought us one thousand six hundred dollars if we sell our catch, and we don't even need to go to the Bank of Scotland to get them," Uncle Tony gave us a broad smile.

"Dad is planning to pay for my school fee with it," Sam said.

"Now, that is exaggerating," Uncle Tony said. "Do you know your grandfather was a legendary fisherman?"

"No. Tell me about it."

"He once caught a Bluefin tuna that sold for a couple of thousands," Uncle Tony said proudly.

Sam and I have never seen our grandad before. I only heard about him from Dad when he told me about it once in a while.

"Why is he so good at it? We want to learn to fish like him too?"

"Your Grandad was a fisherman. He did that for a living. I asked him the same question when I was a kid."

"And what did he say?"

"He said that he can explain it to me all day how a fish bites. But, it is not until I actually catch one, battle with one, and experience the process, I never will learn," Uncle Tony said.

"You never tell us how did Grandad disappear?"

Suddenly, we could feel sadness in his tone.

"Your grandad is a very superstitious man. He believes in Loch Ness Monster actually exist. One night, a circus owner offered a reward of twenty thousand pounds for anyone who could bring the monster to him alive. Every fisherman in town was in mania. Your Grandad and great-uncle were one of them."

"What happened next?"

"I still remember it was a chilly night. Grandad said he would make his name in Loch Ness. He swore to give a better life for us. Then he left with my great-uncle and headed out for the loch. But, they never return. I don't understand what he meant by that. But, now I do."

"Did anyone find Grandad and great-uncle eventually?"

"No. Not at all."

There was a long moment of silence.

"Oh well, enough story for now. I need a beer. Why don't you and Sam have a go and try as well? I will be inside the cabin, if you need me, just give me a yell."

***

"It is going to be a phenomenal night, let's have a competition, shall we?" Sam challenged.

"But…but I am a bit rusty," I choked.

"No, we are descendants of great fishermen," Sam said.

Perhaps Sam is right.

I can learn everything about fishing. But, it is not until I actually catch one, battle with one, and experience the process, I will never learn.

I think I just need a bit more of a practice and more confidence.

The moon hung low in the night sky like a luminous pearl.

Nirvana rocked back and forth along the wave foam crest.

It was rhythmic.

The night of Loch Ness under the reflection of the moonbeam is just scenic.

I glanced around the loch.

It seemed that we are the only one left right now.

The only sound we heard was snoring sound from within the cabin.

Sam and I found a corner on *Nirvana* each.

We hooked our bait and cast our fishing rod.

Howling wind wiped our face.

Soon, *Nirvana* drifted into a curtain of dull mist that partially obliterating our view.

I stared at the black wall of the water.

I wondered what Grandad and great-uncle experience that night in Loch Ness?

What happened to them? Did they get devoured by the storm? Why aren't they found?

My mind was caught in the carousel of thoughts.

Suddenly, a rotten, stomach-churning smell from no-where invaded my nostril.

Oh gross! What is this terrible odour?

Just when I was about to turn to Sam, the fishing reel spun a full turn.

And another…

"Sam," I cried.

Crank Crank Crank

I watched in amazement as the fishing rod continued to blend.

"Reel! Reel! Reel!"

Sam raced over to help.

Even the two of us lifting the fishing rod together with full force. Still, whatever down there was just too strong for us.

"Forget about lifting it up. Keep the tip low, and pull to the side," Sam commanded.

We continued to battle the fish.

The drag was so powerful that we constantly need to resist.

We glanced down at the trophy fish up close as it swam alongside Nirvana.

To be honest, I was a bit freak out when I saw its size.

It was even bigger than the first one we caught.

The fish cleverly dive under *Nirvana*.

"Reel! Reel! Reel!"

"Leon, don't let it a get away! Grab the spear and aim!"

My eyes locked on the murky loch water.

At first, I was fascinated when I saw dozens of slivery salmon with white belly swimming alongside our boat.

Splashing fiercely.

Then something else caught my eyes.

Something that is dark and dull.

Something enormous.

Something reminded me of a giant tadpole lurking beneath our boat...

9

*C*rack!

Without warning, the fishing rod bent in half.

Nirvana tiled left and right.

Ouch!

Sam and I lost our balance and landed on the deck.

Baits laid scattered everywhere.

Even Uncle Tony was awakened by it.

"I…I think I saw something," I stammered.

"Wow, what have you guys done?" Uncle Tony was unimpressed.

"Dad, we almost caught a large salmon or trout and I think our boat hit something," Sam replied.

Uncle Tony searched the murky water with his head torch.

But, there was no sign of any anything.

"I think it is time for us to go home," Uncle Tony said.

"But Dad, we haven't caught anything yet," Sam refused.

"Sam, it is late now. Everyone is tired." Uncle Tony raised his voice.

"Sam, I think we better go. It is almost midnight," I agreed.

"Dad, salmon doesn't rock our boat like that. We hit something...something big. It could be the loch ness monster-" Sam continued.

"Enough monster talk. There is no such thing as Loch Ness Monster. It is not real." Uncle Tony cried angrily.

"So, if it is not the monster, what could hit out boat like that?" Sam argued.

"Whatever it is, it could be anything but the Loch Ness Monster. Now, we go back inside the cabin."

***

Scottish Hearld, March 3rd 2019
Does Monster Really Exist?

After disappearing for a month, there have been sightings of "Long sinuous necks" appearing over the placid waters of the loch. The creature was spotted and photographed by a woman from Manchester on February 23. Lisa and her partner, Danny, were driving near to Urquhart Castle when they made the first February sighting. Lisa's snap shows an L Shaped black object about three feet tall above the water surface, which disappeared into the water shortly after she took the image.

The rooster crowed just before the crack of dawn.

Since six in the morning, Uncle Tony has been grilling the giant Atlantic salmon we caught yesterday.

He seasoned it with lemon slices, brown sugar and salt and sprinkled chopped chives on top.

It tasted absolutely sensational.

I couldn't resist and forked another piece in my mouth.

"Dad, did you read the news? Someone claims they have two sightings in five days!" Sam exclaimed over the breakfast table.

"Well, we got sighting like this all the time. The myth of

the Nessie has captured the imagination of the world for decades." Uncle Tony said.

"In fact, 2017 has been a record year for the sighting of the Loch Ness Monster," I added.

"But, did they found any new solid evidence supporting there is actually a prehistoric dinosaur in Loch Ness," Uncle Tony challenged.

Sam and I shook our heads.

"See, the whole point of these sighting is nothing but for people to cash in on the Loch Ness Monster myth. It is called buy the rumour, sell the news," Uncle Tony continued. "Sam, by now, how many views did your Nessie video hit?"

"Three million,"

"See, that is the point,"

"Uncle Tony, don't you believe in Nessie after living in Scotland all your life?"

"History is riddled with unexplained events. Across the world, there are always claims to sight creatures like Nessie. Crypto-zoologists believe that Nessie might be an isolated pocket of animals thought to have gone extinct." Uncle Tony explained.

"Something like the plesiosaur," Sam added.

"You are right. But the fact is that is Loch Ness is only stretched about twenty-five miles long and one mile in wide. It was covered by glaciers for twenty thousand years and was only formed about ten thousand years ago. Current scientific evidence shows that plesiosaur died out sixty million years ago towards the end of Cretaceous period. Therefore, creature of the size of Nessie would have to enter the loch after the lake was fully formed, and the species would have to live much longer than scientists originally thought, do you think it is possible?"

"It is possible. The new documentary now suggests that T-Rex may have black, bristly tufty of feathers and orange markings around its eyes." Sam defended.

"Assume it is possible. But Loch Ness has limited ecological supplies. Convince me how is that sufficient to support a dinosaur of that size?"

PART 2

10

It has been an ordinary week.

One morning, Uncle Tony left us a message saying he will be in the National Museum of Scotland till late tonight.

He demanded us not to go near the loch without him around.

"Looks like it will only be you and me. Stuck in this big house. No more fishing," I forced a smile.

"I don't think so," Sam giggled.

"What do you mean? Uncle Tony says we can't go into the water. He even locked the boat up," I said.

"Dad won't find out we go into the water unless you tell him," Sam said hastily.

"But, we still need a boat, don't we?" I asked.

"No we don't," Sam grinned.

"I don't quite follow." I was confused.

"Our neighbour, Jimmy, is on school holiday too. His brother has a boat," Sam replied.

"But, it is Jimmy's brother's boat," I said.

"Yes. I know. They texted me asking us if we want to join them today," Sam explained.

"Wow, that is generous of him," I was excited.

"I don't know about that part," Sam said uneasily.

***

We hurried out of the big house.

Above us, the flock of birds flew in the clear blue sky to open the day.

A woodpecker clung to a trunk, tapping the wood rapidly with its beak.

We followed a trail that curved down to a stony creek.

The water was so clear that I could see the bottom.

It was filled with fish.

"Not bad. I don't mind shore fishing in here," I said.

"Don't be silly. Shore fishing is boring. Believe me, it is nowhere near deep-sea fishing." Sam rejected.

"Really? I thought it is the same. You only need a rod." I frowned.

"No. Offshore fishing requires much more than just equipment. You need a large fishing boat. The weather and the time of the year dictate which type of fish you catch. Because we typically catch larger fish, that's why we need expensive equipment and heavy baits. You know, it is heavy-duty. You need a bit of strength." Sam schooled me.

"Make sense." I nodded.

To be honest, I have underestimated the background work Uncle Tony did for us.

"I know how you feel. But, once you have really caught a monster size Atlantic salmon by yourself, you will never go back to shore fishing. It is for babies." Sam spoke like a coach.

"Really? How long it takes you to learn deep-sea fishing?" I asked.

"Well, it takes me one…two of summer school holiday," Sam counted.

"Do you think I will learn it well too?"

"Hey relax, I am sure you will. I am sure."

A moment later, we arrived in front of another holiday house.

Unlike Uncle Tony's house, this one looks less appealing. Broken tiles were everywhere on the roof. The paint was chipped. Everything looked old fashion and poorly maintained. The only thing that caught my eyes was the fishing boat on a trailer was parked outside its front yard.

"Yo, rich Sam. What on earth it takes you so long to come?"

A skinny boy in a jungle hoodie opened the front door and shouted. His eyes were bold. He had a braided hairstyle and chocolate skin. He walked like as if he was playing soft jazz music when he approached us.

"Leon. Jimmy." Sam introduced us.

"Is he your best friend you always talk about?" Jimmy sneered.

"No. He is my cousin." Sam corrected.

"Well, your cousin looks really out of fashion," Jimmy mocked.

"Excuse me?" I said.

Where is this boy's manner?

"Don't worry. Jimmy loves to fool around. He doesn't mean it," Sam tried to ease the tension.

"So, what brought you to my place? Where is your rich Dad?" Jimmy asked.

"Hey, I never say my Dad is rich, okay. He only works in a museum." Sam corrected.

"Sam, do you realize the holiday house you live in is one of the most expensive estates in Loch Ness?" Jimmy asked. "Your dad must be rich."

"Umm… so? Maybe my dad won the lucky draw, God knows." Sam sounded impatient.

"I don't believe in you." Jimmy choked.

"Hello, can we change the subject? What is the agenda for today?" Sam yawned.

"We are heading to the Loch Ness, of course," Jimmy said.

"Great. Sounds like we can go fishing again." I cried happily.

"Huh? Who told you that we are going fishing today?" Jimmy was confused.

"Hello? If we are not going to fish in Loch Ness, what are we doing in the middle of the loch?" I dropped my mouth open.

"I think you have mistaken what we are going to do today." Jimmy grinned.

11

"Hey, Jimmy you little imp, stop fooling around. Get back in the house." A booming voice from inside the house made everyone jumped.

When we turned around, we saw a big guy standing in the doorway. Unlike Jimmy, the guy looked big and muscular. He has big round eyes and braids short hair.

"Not again," Jimmy rolled his eyes.

"Who is he?" I asked.

"This is Tyrone, my brother. He is an undergraduate at the New Zealand University. He doesn't come home usually unless it is semester break," Jimmy said.

"Sorry about my brother's attitude. I am Tyrone, this little imp's brother." Tyrone introduced himself.

"I have already introduced you," Jimmy narrowed his eyes. "What's sup? Big guy."

"Where did you put the car key?" Tyrone questioned.

"God knows where your car key is? I am only twelve. I can't drive. Not yet. Call Mom and Dad." Jimmy burst out.

"So, are you suggesting we are not going to Loch Ness?" Tyrone asked.

"*Nonononono.*" Jimmy pleaded.

"Then get back inside and find it!" Tyrone demanded.

"Fine," Jimmy whined and headed back reluctantly.

A moment later, Tyrone and Jimmy finally found the car key.

Tyrone towed the trailer, secured the load and checked the tires if they are properly inflated.

Jimmy, Sam and I hopped in at the back seat while Tyrone took the wheel.

"Jimmy, why don't you sit next to me?" Tyrone turned his head around and asked.

"You just got your license. I am not that confident about your driving skills." Jimmy teased.

"What did you just say?" Tyrone asked angrily.

Tyrone made a three-point turn and headed towards Loch Ness.

"See. Told you. You have forgotten to signal again."

The tires roared beneath us. The trailer tilted and dipped.

Tyrone and Jimmy argued non-stop the whole trip.

"Hey Tyrone, what you are doing in university?" I asked.

"Well, my major is applied ecology," Tyrone said. He signalled and overtook the car in front of him.

The trailer bounced up and down on the bumpy road.

"Well done," Jimmy teased, playing with his iPhone.

"What is applied ecology about?" Sam pursued.

"Well, we apply the science of ecology to real-world questions. For example, the traditional ways to monitor if a species exist in an area can be expensive and impractical, so what we do is to trace their environmental sample." Tyrone explained.

"How exactly does it work?" I wondered.

"Well, we collect, process and analysis traces of DNA that the species left behind in the environment such as tissues, saliva or freshwater samples. We call it the eDNA sampling." Tyrone continued.

"eDNA sampling?" Jimmy paused his game and raised his ears.

"It means environmental DNA sampling, dopey," Tyrone teased.

Jimmy pretended to be dopey and then continued with his game.

"Wow. Are you proposing we are going to see if the Loch Ness Monster exist by collecting its eDNA?" I speculated.

"Clever." Tyrone appraised. "So far, the evidence of Loch Ness Monster is merely based on blurry photos or cheesy footages. eDNA sampling is a new technique that does not need to harm or disturb the creature and confirm if it exists. In fact, scientists were able to identify six previously unseen species of the shark using eDNA collected in the New Caledonian archipelago in the Pacific Ocean. That is why I have a feeling I am going to be the first to debunk the mystery of Loch Ness scientifically."

***

It was noon.

The golden sky is awash with various shade of grey.

Here we are, in the middle of Loch Ness – the home of a cryptid who has been allegedly sighted by people over the years.

Do you think Loch Ness monster actually does exist? I don't really know.

Some part of me believes what Uncle Tony said. But, on the other hand, I really want it to exist.

After all, there isn't any scientific evidence proving it doesn't, right?

That is what we will discover.

I felt ecstatic.

I wasn't anticipating my hope of going out to fish turned out to become a scientific adventure.

Tyrone called us to get off the car.

He reversed it all the way down the ram until the trailer was in the water.

Jimmy signalled Tyrone when the boat drifts in the trailer.

Tyrone climbed out of the driver seat to unhook the bowel and disengaged the safety strap.

He ordered us to jump in the boat while he parked the car.

"Your brother is good," I appraised.

"If you think he is good now, wait till later. My brother is on the edge of cracking the Loch Ness monster myth. You are in luck today to be a witness," Jimmy said confidently.

"Yo, are you guys ready?" Tyrone's gasping voice called us from behind.

"You have finally done it right. I am impressed," Jimmy said sarcastically.

"Stop talking. Do you have the eDNA kit ready?" Tyrone asked breathlessly.

"Ops, I left it at home," Jimmy pretended.

"You what?"

"Just kidding."

Tyrone fired up the engine and the motor rumbled.

Our boat rocked and tilted.

A Caley Cruisers boat filled with tourists was cruising near the picturesque spot of the Urquhart castle.

"Loch Ness Monster is a business," I recalled my uncle's words.

"Not necessarily," Tyrone shook his head.

"So, you believe in the myth?" Sam's eyes wide open.

Finally, someone is agreeing with him - someone with a science background.

"Have you heard of the Operation Deepscan?" Tyrone asked.

"Never heard of Deepscan before." We shook out head.

"In 1987, a searching team called Deepscan took place in Loch Ness. Twenty four Caley Cruisers boats equipped with sonar were deployed across the whole width of the loch. They simultaneously sent out acoustic waves," Tyrone said.

"Did they find anything unusual?" Our eyes filled with excitement.

"The search lasted for a week and the news reported that a number of sonar contacts had been picked up indicating an unidentified object of unusual size and strength."

Sam and I swallowed hard.

The sky darkened.

The water began to go rough.

The howling wind sang in our ears.

What did Deepscan find? What is that unidentified object he refers to?

12

"What did they find?" We asked impatiently.

"According to the reports, Deepscan proclaimed that after further analysis of the SONAR images, it was concluded that they pointed to debris at the bottom of the lake, although three of the pictures were of moving debris!" Tyrone sounded disappointed.

"What a disappointing conclusion," Jimmy cried in disbelief.

"Did they explain about the moving debris?" I asked, feeling silly.

"Use our imagination," Sam shook his head.

"Don't worry. That is why we are here at this moment – to crack the Loch Ness monster myth." Tyrone encouraged.

"You are right. We will crack the Loss Ness monster myth!" We all agreed.

Tyrone went to his navigator.

He explicitly placed a few markers with different colours on a few locations.

When we asked Tyrone, he said those locations were where people sighted the cryptid in the past. A green marker means the cryptid is sighted once. A red marker represents the cryptid is sighted multiple times in recent years. That way we can streamline our search for the cryptid's eDNA more effectively.

Tyrone stepped on the accelerator.

The engine coughed, leaving traces of bubbles behind.

On our left was a long road that runs along the western shore of Loch Ness.

"Do you know the rumour of the Loch Ness Monster is related to the A82 road?" Tyrone asked.

"No. Tell us about it." I said.

"Strange as it may seem, before 1933, there aren't many sighting of the Loch Ness Monster in Loch Ness. It is only after 1933 when the A82 road is completed, the number of sighting increases significantly. Do you know why?" Tyrone asked.

"Well, when the road is completed, that means more people is able to travel to and from Loch Ness," I guessed.

"But, that still doesn't explain why people's interest in the Loch Ness monster suddenly grew?" Sam defended.

"In 1933, construction began on the A82. Rumours say that because the work requires considerable amount of drilling and blasting, it had disturbed the cryptid from the deep into the open." Tyrone explained.

"Oh, you are right, coincidentally, one year later, R.K. Wilson, the London surgeon, managed to take that photograph showing a slender head and neck rising above the surface of the water," Jimmy exclaimed.

The boat continued to rock and tilt.

Tyrone anchored the boat when we arrived at our first destination. He gave us a DNA extraction kit. Inside were buffering in bottles, sample preparation tubes and strips.

We grabbed a test tube each to collect water samples. The entire process only took us seconds.

"Is that it?" Sam and I were surprised by how easy it was.

"Do you think it will work?" Jimmy doubted.

"Of course. Don't underestimate this. This kit costs thousands." Tyrone said.

"Oh no… I am going to tell Mom and Dad." Jimmy shook his head.

"Say whatever you want. It is my thesis project sponsored by the Natural History Museum." Tyrone said proudly.

"Wow, that is impressive." I applauded. "But, I thought Loch Ness Monster belongs to Scotland. What does it have to do with the Natural History Museum?"

"I care less. It is none of my business. I only need the funding for my research," Tyrone said coldly. "Now, are we done yet in this spot?"

Dusk faded in slowly as the sky turned from grey to black.

The Caley Cruisers boat we saw in the afternoon was on their return trip.

We have been circling around Loch Ness the whole afternoon to collect samples at the marked spots.

But, there are still a few spots we missed.

"Hey, Tyrone, it is dark. Should we go? I worry that Dad will be back and realize we are not here?" Sam asked.

Tyrone ignored him.

He continued to sail further to the next marked destination.

Huh? What is wrong with him?

"Hey, Jimmy, is there something wrong?" I whispered.

"My brother has a strange habit." Jimmy giggled.

"What is it?"

"He always insists to finish what he set off to do that day." Jimmy laughed.

Huh? Does that mean we are not going home unless he finishes?

Sam's mobile rang nonstop.

It was Uncle Tony calling.

"Oh no, it is Dad," Sam and I exchanged a worry glance.

"Hey Tyrone, can we just go?" I demanded.

Tyrone stopped sailing. He turned to me and gave me the nastiest look I have even seen.

"No one is stopping you from leaving. You can swim all the way to the shore if you wish."

13

"You...you are scaring us," My voice came out trembling.

"You are scaring us," Jimmy mimicked. "No one invites you to come with us."

"Sam?" I turned to my cousin.

"Jimmy, what is wrong with you? Why so mean?" Sam protested.

"We are not mean." Jimmy shook his head.

A moment later, the weather changed.

Soft, steady rain whipped our face.

The wind was screaming like a banshee.

Bolts of lightning cracked the inky sky.

"My brother is very passionate about his work. No one can stop him, not even the thunder and the rain," Jimmy laughed.

"This is insane," I condemned.

"I am going to call dad back," Sam tried to answer the phone.

But, suddenly, Tyrone stepped on the accelerator.

The momentum caught Sam off-guard. His mobile slipped from his hand and sank into the depth of the loch.

"Hey!" Sam shouted.

"Oops, we are sorry," Jimmy pretended.

I felt regret. We should have listened to Uncle Tony and stayed home. Right now, we are risking our life with two evil people nowhere in the loch.

"If Dad finds out, you will be in serious trouble," Sam accused.

"Oh please, we are so scared. By the way, who knows you come and visit us today? How about if your dad never finds out." Jimmy pretended.

"What …what do you mean he never finds out?" Sam and I stammered.

"What if you had an accident? What if you stumbled into the Nessie and it pulled you all the way down in the depth of Loch Ness? After all, it was always you who is obsessed with the Loch Ness Monster." Jimmy kept imagining.

The thunder rolled across the malevolent sky.

A bolt of white lightning jagged the utter blackness.

It revealed the laughing Jimmy.

His evil laugh reminded us of the Joker in Batman movies.

Then something caught the corner of our eyes.

Something moving swiftly in the black water…

Something with black humps, tail, and snake-like head.

Is it a tree log? Is it a seal? Is it simply a trick of the light?

I don't know.

But, it doesn't take long for me to find out.

Before I could react, I saw it behind Jimmy.

I saw a mysterious huge shadow with a long neck flashed behind the brilliant shock of white.

14

"Look out!" Sam cried on top of his lung as our boat bumped right into the creature.

Tyrone decelerated to a halt.

"I can't believe it! We collide with the elusive fake submerged Nessie toy figure!" Tyrone roared, feeling stupid.

Behind us, a team of Scottish police boat was horning, calling us to stop.

"What a coincident!" Jimmy was shocked when he saw the police.

Sam and I exchanged a glance with each other.

"Oops, it looks like we are in serious trouble."

***

"Sam, what on earth were you thinking?" Uncle Tony scolded when we get back to the house.

"I...I," Sam stammered.

"How many times do I have to tell you to stay away from Jimmy and his family?" Uncle Tony asked.

"Dad, I am sorry, I just don't want Leon to stay home all day, we want to go fishing at the beginning and - "

"No, you are not. The police said the four of you are

collecting eDNA samples from Loch Ness." Uncle Tony interrupted. "How many times do I have to repeat myself again that the monster does not exist."

"But, it is the truth! We only find out they are not going there to fish later on." Sam defended. "What is wrong with doing a scientific experiment?"

"The experiment you friends are doing has already been done by universities. I am not against you doing a fun science project. But, you are jeopardizing your safety. And more importantly, your cousin's safety."

"Sorry, Uncle Tony," I apologized. "Sam is right. We only found out about that later. We…we don't do it again. I promise."

Uncle Tony took a deep breath and said. "Leon. Sam. No more Nessie from now on. Promised?"

"We promise."

The next morning, Uncle Tony was gone again.

He told us that some major event is happening in the museum that he is occupied.

Fair enough.

But, that means we won't be fishing again today.

"Do you think Tyrone's eDNA kit could really have some breakthrough?" Sam wondered.

"Sam, you are not going to contact them again, are you?" I asked.

"Definitely not, but I am just curious," Sam shied away, undecided.

"They are dangerous. I can't imagine what will happen to us if the police hadn't come just in time." I said.

"Yes. About the police, do you think it is a coincident the police found us?" Sam wondered.

"Hmmm, you are right. How did the police know we

were there?" I felt suspicious.

We continued with our never-ending conversation until our mouth went dry.

Sam dashed to the kitchen and grabbed me a can of coke.

"Hey Leon, do you want to check out my cinema room and watch a movie or two?" Sam suggested.

"You have a cinema room? Why don't you show it to me earlier?" I was impressed.

"It is because you never ask."

Uncle Tony's holiday house is truly amazing.

It has an open layout cinema room. The grey carpet, the crystal lamp and the sofa in the room made everything looked expensive.

And I haven't even talked about the seventy-five-inch wall-mounted television yet!

I wonder how long Sam hasn't been to the movies.

Sam has shown me the movies he got.

Then he raced off again.

"Where are you going?" I asked.

"To make some popcorn, of course. How could we watch movies without caramel popcorns?"

I scrolled down the list of all the latest movies in Sam's TV box. Undecided. It looks like there are a lot of new ones for me.

When Sam is done, the two of us were hugging family size popcorn each while enjoying the movie.

"Nice to see there aren't trailers like that in cinema," I joked.

Half an hour passed, we couldn't take our eyes off the big screen.

Suddenly, the air was rented by the banging sound from

inside the house.

Sam and I exchanged a worry glance. We turned the television volume down. We raised our ears, listening like bunnies.

"What is that?" I whispered nervously.

"I...I don't know. Someone knocked down something." Sam stammered.

"Hang on, but there is no one else besides us in the house." I swallowed hard.

The banging sound came again.

This time is louder and clearer.

"Weird, it looks like it is coming from downstairs," Sam speculated.

"Is it a thief? Is it Tyrone or Jimmy? Should we call the police? Or should we call Uncle Tony?" I kept asking.

I tried to stay calm. But, I simply couldn't. Not in a big house like this. Not when we expect to be the only ones in the house.

"Let's go and check it out," Sam suggested.

Is Sam okay? What if it is dangerous? What if it is a robbery?

"Sam? I don't think it is such a good idea," I declined.

"Don't worry. It is my house. I live here," Sam insisted.

I had no choice but to follow. Reluctantly.

Sam and I tiptoed to his room to get a baseball bat.

We tried to be as stealthy as possible.

The banging sound happened again.

"Strange, it doesn't seem to be coming from the kitchen," Sam whispered.

"Not from the kitchen? Then where else could it be?" I asked.

"No idea." Sam shrugged.

We cautiously descended the carpeted spiral stairs.

The sitting room looked tidy.

We searched for the other place downstairs meticulously.

No one is there. No moved furniture. All the doors and windows are locked.

Are we just hearing things?

"Maybe we watch too many movies. We can't find even a shard of glass in here," I uttered a sigh of relieve.

"Maybe it is just our imagination? God. I have never scared ourselves like this in my life." Sam wiped the river of sweat in his forehead.

Just as we were about to relax and get back upstairs, a strange squishing sound from the basement made our adrenalin rush.

The next thing I heard was our screams.

15

"It…it comes from the…the basement?" I stammered.

"But, the basement supposed to be a storeroom. Dad said it is scattered with abandoned furniture, nuts and bolts." Sam remembered.

"Nuts and bolts don't make a sound like this, do they?" I corrected.

"Obviously not. Unless they behave like in the Toy Story. Should we check it out?" Sam asked boldly.

"But, Uncle Tony asks us to stay out of the basement," I warned.

"There is a strange sound in my house giving me creeps. I can't stand it. I really want to find it out," Sam said sharply.

"Okay. Okay," I replied. "But, the basement is locked at all times."

"We will need to find the key. But, the problem is that Dad always keeps the basement key with him the whole time," Sam sounded troubled. He crossed his arms, trying to think.

"How about – " I kept thinking.

"I am listening," Sam said.

"How about we lock pick?" I suggested reluctantly, feeling guilty.

One part of me really wants to discover what's behind that door. Another part of me can't imagine how Uncle Tony will feel if he found out we entered his basement like this.

The two of us searched YouTube.

We studied how people use tension wrench and apply torque back and forth, and repeats.

Sam and I spent the next half an hour search the house for the tool.

But we can't find anything that fits.

"Looks like we have no luck with it." I sighed.

Just when we were about to give up, Sam snatched the handle slammed the door with one shoulder.

To our surprise, the door crashed open in the blink of an eye!

It wasn't even locked!

"Sam, are you okay?" I tried to help Sam as he staggered a few steps forward.

"I… I am fine," Sam said as he got back up to his feet.

The basement felt somewhat stagnant.

Cold air from within made both of us shivered.

Just by viewing from the gap of the basement door, the interior of the basement looked more industrial-like.

It had stonewalled on both sides. The floor was a seamless metal grid.

We tried to feel for the light switch, but it was just too dark to see.

"Found it," Sam spoke eventually.

When Sam switched the light on, we were astonished by what we saw under the dim light.

"What a mess! Dust everywhere!" Sam coughed. He complained when we saw abandoned furniture everywhere.

"Careful, there might be bolts, nuts and broken glasses on the floor," Sam warned.

"No worries."

I cautiously walked around the furniture.

Look! Here is the cupboard that Sam used to have in his old holiday house.

Now it is all covered with spider webs.

"Oh my god, here is my war hammer figure collection. I wonder where they were all these times!" Sam exclaimed.

We searched everywhere.

But, there were still no traces of the banging or the squishing sound.

Then we heard the dripping water sound between the cracks of the stone.

"Water?" I pressed my ears against the stonewall and listened.

The sound of running water was crystal clear.

"Hey Sam, come and listen," I called.

"Strange." Sam narrowed his eyebrow. "I never hear water sound inside the house."

"What does this mean?" I asked.

"That means the house may be connected to the loch." Sam hypothesized.

"A house connecting to the loch? It doesn't make any sense." I said.

The two of us continued our search.

Sam was excited as some of the things brought back his memories.

"I can't believe Dad is storing so many rubbish in the

basement. It is like one large dusty rubbish bin." Sam complained.

"Okay. Seems like nothing unusual in here except rubbish." I concluded.

"Maybe we are just hearing things in this big house." Sam gave the basement one last look, turned around, and said. "Let's leave."

Coo. Coo.

A strange voice from the basement stopped us, followed by a strange squishing sound, and then silence again.

"Sam...did you hear that too?"

"We are definitely not imagining things. There is something inside the basement."

Our eyes darted left and right.

But, there was nothing else beside furniture.

We walked back into where the sound came from.

We couldn't believe our eyes when we saw it.

A trapdoor.

16

Sam and I were stunned.

I don't know how long Sam has been in this holiday house, but it looks like a discovery for him.

Do you have such experience?

Imagine, one day, you realize your house is actually bigger than you thought.

Imagine, one day, you accidentally discovered an unexplored dungeon or peculiar room below your house.

This is exactly what is happening to us right now.

How intriguing.

"Sam, are we going down?" I asked. My voice came out trembling.

Sam nodded. He looked solemn.

We opened the creaking trapdoor and lowered ourselves down the ladder.

Since the ladder was short, we hopped down when we almost reached the last few steps.

The air felt humid and chilly.

The water dripping sound was crystal clear.

When we landed, we found ourselves in another room.

Unlike the upper level, this one is much tidier. There

are even toilets in here.

"What the –" I opened my mouth but no sound came out.

It looks like Uncle Tony deliberately wants to hide this place.

The stonewall was pinned with an oversized board.

In the middle of the room was a large, square table with a sophisticated computer. Light bulbs in suspension cord were swinging back and forth on the ceiling.

Beside the computer were racks of empty test tubes with Genesis's logo on them.

A flask with a pink solution was placed underneath a burette.

It still felt warm.

"What on earth is Dad doing in here?" Sam spoke, his eyes wild opened in disbelief.

"It looks like Uncle Tony is doing some kind of experiment." I guessed.

"Careful. Broken glass on the floor." Sam alerted me.

I cautiously walked to the table.

It seems that Uncle Tony was scribbling of some kind of chemical formula on paper.

I wonder what is he experimenting on.

I randomly picked up one of the testing records.

The date was yesterday night at three!

Did Uncle Tony spend all night here?

Step by step, Sam cautiously walked to the rows of lockers.

Beside the lockers was an oversized board on the wall.

Below the board was a drawer tool chest with torch, spanners and drills.

Interesting enough, the board was pinned with news

and photos about the cryptid Uncle Tony declined it exists.

"Four Sundays ago after church I went for my usual walk near where the river enters the Loch. The Loch was like a millpond and the sun shining brightly. An object of considerable dimensions rose out of the water not very far from where I was. I immediately got my camera ready and snapped the object which was two or three feet above the surface of the water. I did not see any head, for what I took to be the front parts were under the water, but there was considerable movement from what seemed to be the tail, the part furthest from me. The object only appeared for a few minutes then sank out of sight."

Some of the news was dated back to 1933.

Another news dated on April 25, 1977. It was a black and white photo showing a giant carcass with four paddle-like limbs and long neck, netted by a Japanese trawler, hoisted above the deck of a Japanese fishing vessel.

It looks like Uncle Tony is obsessed with the Loch Ness Monster legend.

Look! There is a map that red-circled with the location where the cryptid had been sighted over the years!

Apparently, Uncle Tony is secretly investigating it.

But why is he spending so much effort on something he insisted does not exist?

I walked over to a cupboard.

Inside were formaldehyde-filled jars of dissected fish and organs.

They looked so well preserved.

My heart almost skipped a beat when I saw a chameleon-fish hybrid in a formalin jar.

Yuck! What on earth is that!

Coo. Coo. Coo. Coo.

The mysterious sound sent chills down our spine.

Sam and I looked at each other in fright.

What on earth is Uncle Tony doing?

We turned to our left and saw a sturdy silvery door that was left half-open.

"Whatever making the sound should be behind that door," Sam said quietly.

The two of us swallowed hard.

Sweat was raining down our forehead.

We held our baseball bat tight, ready to smash if anything attacks.

"Leon, are you ready?"

"One."

"Two"

"Three."

17

We pushed the creaking door opened with all our strength.

Immediately, a disguising odour invaded our nostril.

"Yuck. It smells like sewage or something?" I choked, complaining.

Our mouth dropped open in surprise when we saw the secret behind the door.

It...it was no room. No lab.

Basically, we found ourselves on a platform with a short ram that led to a dark, endless subterranean lake!

Next to the ram was a small yellow boat floating on the dark green water, anchored to a hook through a rope.

Huh? An... an endless subterranean lake?

"The place is warm, humid and stink. And it is too dark to see." I complain.

"Here, grab the torch," Sam handed me a torch he found on Uncle's Tony's drawer tool chest earlier.

"Do you have some kind of gas mask with a filter too?" I asked.

"Unfortunately, Dad didn't keep any gas mask," Sam declined.

I wonder how he can endure the bad odour.

The circle of light from our torches randomly darted left and right in the darkness.

Even with a high-intensity flashlight, our beam was swallowed up by the darkness long before it could reach the far wall or ceiling.

It looked like the subterranean lake stretched all the way to infinity.

Is that even possible?

"I guess you are right, your holiday house is really connected to the loch," I said, shielding my nose and mouth.

"I think Dad has got quite a lot to explain," Sam whispered.

"By the way, do you think Uncle Tony knows it when he bought the holiday house?" I asked.

"I have no idea. I don't think this gone through a real estate agent or conveyancer," Sam said.

"Weird, I think the conveyance would have picked this up when they looked at the floor plan and strata," I guessed.

"The house has no strata. It is a house, remember?" Sam corrected. "One day, Dad came home and just told us he bought a new holiday house. That's it."

"So, Aunty Belly didn't know this either?" I was amused.

"Nope. Dad kept everything to himself lately," Sam replied.

He hopped on the small yellow boat, and stinky water splashed all over me.

"Hey," I yelled.

"Sorry," Sam apologized. He staggered a little bit as the small yellow boat rocked left and right.

I checked the time on my iPhone.

It was almost four o' clock.

"Sam. We better go. We have seen enough for today," I suggested.

"Are you kidding? Where is that Leon I used to know? The one with an adventurous spirit." Sam teased.

"But, Sam, no one knows we went down here. There is no reception on our phone. There is no –"

"Leon, are you scare?"

"No…Of course not."

"We are not going to stay here for a very long time. Just one round trip and we will go back up."

I know what Sam is thinking.

Mysteries were circling in our head like a carousel.

We really want to find out what is going on. We really do.

"Just one round trip, deal?" I finally spoke.

"Deal." Sam agreed.

I hopped in next to Sam.

The two of us grabbed the paddle and began to sail.

The dark green water was murky and thick, like green pea soup.

Sam leaned down to get a better look.

I could hear its gurgling and plopping sound as it churned.

Strange.

I raise my head to look at the ceiling.

Apparently, it is a subterranean cave filled with uneven stone column and stalactites.

We continued to paddle.

The periodic water dripping sound was crystal clear.

The short ram and the entrance where we came in

slowly disappeared from view.

Our yellow boat dodged passes a stalagmite into an even larger, wider opening.

"It looks like the subterranean lake could lead us right back to the loch," I speculated.

"Yes. Perhaps it could lead us to an unexplored part of the Loch Ness," Sam added.

"Do you think Uncle Tony really believes the Loch Ness Monster doesn't exist?" I asked.

"I don't know what Dad is thinking. All I know is that he is hiding something…something he doesn't want the world to know," Sam replied.

"Do you think it has to do with our grandad and great-uncle?" I guessed.

"Possibly. Dad always tells me stories about how grandad disappeared that night when he searched for the Loch Ness Monster. Maybe Dad can't get over it even after so many years. And Mom gets mad about him when he talks about it to me," Sam said.

"Hey, this is exactly what my parents did! Mom keeps on telling Dad not to tell me those wild stories," I agreed.

Splash! Splash!

Suddenly, a splashing sound from nowhere interrupted us.

"Who…who is that?" My voice came out trembling.

Our spotlight danced randomly on the murky, green water surface.

But, we could see nothing, but ripples that remained.

"Huh? We certainly heard something splashing," I insisted.

"Maybe rock sediments fall from the top," Sam explained.

Splash! Splash!

The water splashed again.

This time it just happened meters from our small boat.

"Over there! Over there!" I cried repeatedly.

I shone my torch to the water.

Chill ran down my spine when I spotted something that reminded me of a lizard belly.

The beige figure squirmed and slithered on the water surface momentarily, splashed and disappeared in the murky green soup again.

I opened my mouth but no sound came out.

"What is that? Where is it?" Sam turned to me.

But, he was too slow.

There was nothing but murky green.

My eyes locked on the water surface.

Drops of sweat rained down from my forehead.

I definitely saw something.

Coo. Coo.

A familiar sound echoed loudly in the opening.

"Sam, let's get out of here!" I shrieked.

Just as we were about to turn back, we saw strange wave formation swimming in our direction like a sequence of bumps.

"Sam!" I whined. My fingers numbed.

My heartbeats quickened.

My mind was racing.

What could possibly lurk in this murky lake? How big is it? Will it eat us alive?

I watched closely as the dark figure crept along the dark water surface.

Closer and closer.

"Sam? Hurry!" My voice came out trembling.

"What is it?"

"I…I don't know. But, whatever it is, it is swimming right towards us. And it is fast!"

We paddled with all our strength.

Then we saw the light from the far end.

"Leon, look! The exit!" Sam cried happily.

Just when we were about to relieve, a shadowy figure leapt out from the greenish water made both of us jump.

18

"*Noooooooooo!*"

We closed our eyes, cried and trashed our arm in the air like madmen.

When we reopened our eyes again, we saw was a cute creature the size of a puppy.

The creature has a long neck, like a snake. It has a board, a flat body and four long flippers. Its tail bore a vertical fin. Its skin is smooth like seal, dark blue on top, grading to light grey underneath.

It blinked at the two idiots waving and screaming. Confused.

Then it splashed itself dry like a puppy.

Coo. Coo.

It cried.

I rubbed my eyes and squinted down at it.

The creature's two, round black eyes blinked at me.

Am I seeing things?

Am I really looking at a plesiosaur that lives and breath?

"Wow, a baby plesiosaur," Sam exclaimed.

The creature pulled itself forward with its front flippers

and cried.

"Oh my god, it looks so cute." I giggled, couldn't believe my own eyes.

I reached out to touch its small head.

It obediently lowered its head.

Then we heard its stomach growled.

"Is…is it hungry?" I asked.

Coo. Coo.

"Wait, let's take it back to the lab, I am sure Dad must have kept some food inside for it," Sam said. Excited.

We sailed back to anchor the boat.

To my surprise, the baby plesiosaur leapt to the ram and slid up as if this is its home.

"Wow, that's smart. I think it has been trained," Sam said gleefully.

"Hey wait up, a little plesiosaur."

The little creature slid smoothly and disappeared behind the sturdy silvery door.

We followed it from behind but it was too agile for us.

"Where did it go?" Sam looked everywhere in the lab.

But the creature is nowhere to be seen.

"Wow, I can't believe we lost it right before our eyes," I said.

Coo. Coo.

The creature's cry drew our attention to a cupboard in the left-hand side of the lab.

When we finally spot it, it was already sliding towards a tall blue bucket in the corner of the room.

Bump! Bump!

The creature bumped the bucket repeatedly. It turned to us, and then bumped the blue bucket again.

"It looks like it wants to show us something," I said.

Sam and I hurried to the tall blue bucket.

We lowered our head and peered down inside the blue bucket.

It was filled with fish.

I see. That's what it is asking us to do.

Sam and I grabbed some and threw it to the creature.

The creature flexed its long neck and devoured it with agility.

"Wow, cool!" Sam was impressed.

He grabbed a few more fish and hung it high above it.

The creature leapt high in the air and took them away in the blink of an eye.

"It is fast. Real fast. I am impressed," I said.

"Me too," Sam agreed.

The two of us cried gleefully while playing with the creature.

"What should we call it?" Sam asked.

Coo. Coo.

"Since it is always making this sound. Should we call it *Coo*?" I suggested.

"*Coo*. Not bad as a name." Sam agreed.

We continued to feed it without realizing we almost emptied the blue bucket.

"Ops, Uncle Tony will find it out we have been feeding *Coo*." I realized.

"You are right. We are too excited. Isn't this right, *Coo*?" Sam asked and looked at the little creature.

"Do we have some fish left in the fridge upstairs?" I asked.

"Oh yes. Nice idea, maybe we can just replace it and pretend nothing happened." Sam agreed.

"Cool. Sam, you stay with *Coo*. I am going to get it."

I climbed back up the small ladder and exited the trap-door.

I tiptoed back outside the basement door.

And *BUMP!*

I bumped right into a tall man with an iconic horseshoe moustache.

My eyes were wide open with fright.

Is that who I think it is?

Before I could speak, the man lowered his head and asked. "What are you doing in my basement?"

19

"Ouch, Dad, it hurts. Let me explain." Sam whined as Uncle Tony pinched his ears all the way back up in the sitting room.

"What else do you have to explain?" Uncle Tony released him, arm folded.

"Leon and I were just watching TV when we heard the banging sound downstairs. We thought there is a break in so we investigate!" Sam cried.

"And you checked everywhere and discovered there is no thief. So, you disobeyed me and headed down to the basement to find out what I am up to," Uncle Tony accursed.

"No. Uncle Tony, we heard a strange sound from the basement." I defended.

Uncle Tony stared at the two of us.

Then he rolled his eyes and uttered a long sigh.

"We are sorry," Sam and I apologized. "We don't mean to –"

Uncle Tony stopped us before we say anything more.

"I am a sorry kid. I am sorry." Uncle Tony spoke.

Then we saw *Coo* appeared from behind the basement door.

"Dad is...is *Coo* the legendary Loch Ness Monster," Sam asked in a low voice.

Uncle Tony gazed at the baby plesiosaur, turned to us, and looked at the baby plesiosaur again.

"Dad?"

Uncle Tony nodded.

"Perhaps I should start right from the beginning."

PART 3

1933

20

"Michael, we must retreat back to the shore before the storm hits!" Owen's voice came out muffled as if carried away by the wind.

The sky darkened.

Bolts of lightning cracked the inky sky.

Angry choppy waves echoed across the gigantic loch, rolling in and out.

Michael ignored his brother.

Although every cell in his body is screaming at him to turn back, he persisted.

"No. We must press on. There is no turning back now," Michael turned to Owen.

Continuous icy rain pattered on their face.

Heavier and heavier.

"Are you crazy! Are you risking our life for a mere legend?" Owen protested.

The wind rose again.

Tall foam waves towered over their helpless yellow boat.

The seagulls above their head were like tossed paper caught in the storm, struggling against the gale.

"It is no legend. It is right beneath the loch. I knew it."

Michael insisted.

"Please. I just want to go home. Please," Owen pleaded.

No matter how hard Owen tried, his stubborn brother turned a deaf ear to all sign of warnings.

Thunders cracked the ominous black clouds.

The wave grew mountainous that their boat was dwarfed, riding up and down like child's toy.

"Look out!"

Before Owen could react, Michael slipped on the wave soaked deck.

Crack!

"Ouch! I broke my ankle. I broke my ankle. Pain. Pain," Michael clenched his teeth.

Owen hurried to help his brother.

"Are...are you all right? Can you stand up?" Owen stammered.

Michael tried but the pain was unbearable.

"No. I am afraid I have to count on you now," Michael's expression turned grimace.

"But, I... I can't paddle. I ...I don't even know the way. What shall we do? What shall we do?" Owen panicked.

"You have to try!" Michael roared.

Lightning struck once more.

A mysterious huge shadow with a long neck flashed behind the brilliant shock of white in the graphite sky.

"Mi...Michael! Did...did you see that?"

"See what!"

"That!"

Owen pointed to the whipping neck behind them. It has a small head with needle-toothed jaws.

"Oh my God, is that what I think it is? Is...is it the legendary sea serpent!" Michael squinted above, his mouth dropped open.

Excited, but fear.

He cried and thrashed his arms fancily in the air, "Brother, we see it. We finally see it! This time we are going to be rich! We are going to be rich!"

Another wave-tossed their boat high.

They were completely soaked.

Before Owen could react, his brother slipped.

The next thing he heard was Michael's scream trailed off as he was thrashed right into the loch!

"*Noooooooo*!" Owen cried on top of his lung.

He tried to reach out for his brother, but it was too late.

Desperate. Fear. Sorrow.

Owen collapsed onto the deck, giving in to the hostile weather.

Soon, he let go of the rail too…

Until something wet looped around his body…

And dragged him into the loch…

Down and down into the dreadful deep…

***

Myriad of bird sang in the cloudless blue sky.

The rhythm percussion wave crashed into the rock platform and retreated, leaving behind a long white fringe.

Stretch of warm golden beam enveloped Owen's body as he began to wake up.

Slowly, Owen opened his eyes.

A large figure with a long neck towered over him.

He raised his head. He rubbed his knuckled onto his eye to make sure he is not just seeing things.

"*Noooooooooooooo*!" Owen screamed in horror when the

large figure lowered its head to lick him. His whole body trembled.

"Get away from me! Get away from me!"

Owen cried repeatedly, eyes closed.

The poor man waited for the creature to attack.

Seconds passed. Then minutes.

Nothing happened.

Owen opened one of his eyes. He saw the creature smiled at him.

Next to the creature was his wrecked boat.

"You…you saved my life?" Owen's voice came out shaking.

The creature nodded.

"You…you understand me?" Owen wondered.

Happy, but confused.

"I do not only understand you. I can speak English," The creature spoke.

"You speak English?" Owen dropped his mouth opened.

"Yes. I do. I speak Scottish English, Gaelic and many European languages. Bonjour!" The creature cried.

"Bonjour!" Owen smiled.

Owen stared at the mighty creature.

So, the legend is true. Loch Ness Monster really exists. And it speaks English.

"What is your name?" Owen asked.

"You can call me like what others call me. You can call me Nessie." Nessie spoke.

"How do you know we call you Nessie?" Owen was impressed.

"I know many other things you don't know about," Nessie giggled. "By the way, little people, what is your name?"

"Owen," Owen said. His fear slowly extinguished. It looked like the creature is not only friendly but has a sense of humour as well.

"Owen," Nessie said thoughtfully. "It is a boring name."

Hey, hang on a second. Where is Michael?

Owen turned around. It looked like he is in some kind of island.

"Stranger. I have never seen this place before," Owen muttered.

By the way, where is my brother?

"Michael! Where are you?" Owen cried on top of his lung.

But, it looked like there is no other human except him.

"Have you seen my brother?" Owen asked the creature.

"Yes. I did. Unfortunately, I didn't manage to save him. The storm dragged him away," Nessie sighed.

Owen collapsed onto his knees. Defeated.

"Why are you crying?" Nessie asked.

"I lost my brother." Owen sobbed.

Nessie tried to soothe Owen with its flippers, but it got its friend all wet.

"Ops," It said, and shied away.

There was a long moment of silence.

"I know how you feel. I once lost someone important too. So, I know how you feel." Nessie tried to break the ice.

Owen and the legendary creature stared out at the crimson morning sky.

Mellow blues and pinks blurred together to create another gorgeous scene.

The orange-hued rays disappeared behind the puffy

cloud momentarily and reappeared again.

Owen raised his head to look at the mythical creature he dreamt of.

A strange mixture of emotions heaved inside him.

Everything looked so real.

But, everything looked so unreal.

He felt sorrow about losing his brother.

He wanted to get back to see his family.

But, on the other hand, he wishes time would halt.

21

Owen followed Nessie as it led him along the shoreline.

The trail curved into an opening, that sloped upwards to a rocky ledge.

The creature pulled itself forward with its front flippers.

"Wait! You are too fast!" Owen shouted, lagging behind.

Nessie laughed. It slid even quicker to the edge of a ledge, dived and disappeared behind in the water.

"Hey, where are you going?" Owen asked.

He carefully looked down the ledge.

He could see nothing but the crashing waves.

There were no signs of Nessie.

"Nessie!" Owen yelled.

"Looking for me?"

When Owen turned around, he saw Nessie carrying a mouthful of fish.

"Wow, how did you come back up so quick?" Owen was amazed.

"Of course. It is my playground." Nessie laughed again.

"Here, catch."

It dropped a fish for Owen. It was a snapper.

"I am feeding the rest to my little one," Nessie said.

"You … you have a child?" I was amused.

"Yes. He is my little boy. His name is *Coo*." Nessie said.

Owen and Nessie continued to march up the rocky ledge.

When they reached the top, they followed a trail that curved downhill into the opening of a basalt shore cave.

"Welcome to my home," Nessie gestured Owen to come over with its flipper.

Owen carefully jumped from one boulder to another.

The entrance of the cave had a passage that branches into any others.

"Why do you keep your child here?" Owen asked.

"Because this is the only safe place on this island," Nessie said sadly.

"What do you mean?" Owen frowned.

Nessie motioned to the sky above.

The flock of birds flew high in the sky.

"Just birds. What is so special?" Owen squinted at the sky.

But it was too bright to see anything clear.

"No. They are not just birds. They are pterosaurs."

***

Owen followed Nessie inside the cave.

The water was high.

Eventually, Owen gave up on walking and climbed onto Nessie's back.

"Wow, your skin is so smooth," Owen appraised.

He felt the Nessie's gigantic body heaved rhythmically

up and down when it breathes.

Perhaps he is the first man ever to ride a dinosaur.

It felt so incredible. It felt so special. It felt so unreal.

"Hold on tight," Nessie warned.

It dived into the green murky water to avoid the stone columns and stalactites.

When it resurfaced again, they are in another section of the sea cave.

Owen coughed and complained. "I didn't expect you to dive."

"Sorry."

The periodic water dripping sound sang in the background.

"*Coo Coo. Coo Coo.*" Nessie sang.

Owen was dumbfounded when he saw was a cute creature the size of a puppy.

The creature has a long neck, like a snake. It has a board, a flat body and four long flippers. Its tail bore a vertical fin. Its skin is smooth like seal, dark blue on top, grading to light grey underneath.

When it saw Owen, it quickly slid to hide behind its mother.

"*Coo.* It is okay. Easy. My little boy." Nessie licked *Coo* clean.

It dropped the mouthful of fish onto the ground.

And *Coo* began to feed.

Owen watched quietly at the mothering behaviour of this legendary beast.

There is so much love. There is so much care.

It is the same beast that saved his life in the storm.

It is the same beast that could earn him twenty thousand pounds if he brings it back alive.

Then he began to regret.

"I vow to keep the secret of Nessie until my very last breath."

22

Time passed like flying colour.

Owen lost track of the time since he landed on this island.

Am I still in Scotland? Where am I? How can I get home? How can I get back to my wife and kids?

He has been out for too long.

His family is waiting for him to come home.

"Nessie, am I still in Loch Ness?" Owen asked.

"Loch Ness? Do you mean the tiny pond that barely has any fish to eat?" Nessie asked.

"Umm… I suppose we are talking about the same place," Owen scratched his head.

"I don't live there. I just visit there sometimes," Nessie laughed.

"What do you mean?" Owen asked.

"Well, the bottom of Loch Ness branches out to different canals deep in the ocean. Many of them led to uncharted landmass or deeper ocean. I live wherever I feel safe."

"The world thought you are indigenous in Loch Ness. That is why we call you the Loch Ness Monster," Owen exclaimed.

"No. I think you have it all wrong. I roamed the ocean deep. And Loch Ness is just a place I come up to take a breath." Nessie explained.

"People believe you are a myth. They think that you are the only remaining dinosaur that exists," Owen felt relieved.

"Is that so?" Nessie forced a smile. "I wish I am the only remaining dinosaur so that I don't need to hide."

"Hide from what?"

THUD THUD THUD

The ceiling of the sea cave was thumping above our head like a giant walk pass.

The rocks sediments from above the cave shook and fell.

"Look out!"

Nessie roared when a large chunk of stalactite fell right in front of them, into the water, sending splashes everywhere.

"What...what was that?" Owen stammered.

"This island is not as safe as you think. Prehistoric dinosaurs roamed the land freely. Perhaps it is time for me to move my nest to somewhere safe," Nessie said.

23

"Uncle Tony, what happens next?" I asked.

Sam and I were raising our ears like bunnies as we listened to Uncle Tony's peculiar story.

"Your grandad disappeared for almost a year. Your grandmother was crying every night. Your father and I had no choice but to carry on the fishing business. Just when everyone thought your grandad was dead, one night, he returned home."

***

One fine afternoon, Tony and Wilson came back from fishing.

As usual, they were empty hand.

They exclaimed at the horizon of the sea.

"Life is so difficult," Tony sighed.

"Don't worry. God closes a door and he opens a window." Wilson soothed his brother.

They lied on the sand and waited until sunset.

The sky was crimson pink.

Waves were racing to crash into the rock and boulders.

Just when they were about to leave, from the corner of their eyes, they saw a figure staggering out of the sea cave from their left.

"Hey, Tony, does that man looks like Dad?" Wilson pointed to the man and asked.

Tony cupped his eyes with his hands and squinted into the distance.

At that moment, the two boys couldn't believe their eyes.

"Oh my god. Yes...Yes. It is Dad!"

The two boys raced towards the filthy man.

"Dad, you...you are alive?"

Even from a distance, they could see their dad's shirts were badly torn. There were wounds everywhere. They could smell the bad odour that reminded them of swarms.

Owen looked at his long lost family staggering towards them.

"Dad, where have you been in the entire year?"

"Why don't you come back? How could you leave us just like that?"

They sobbed and complained.

Emotions heaved in their shoulders.

Then they noticed something else.

Their dad was cradling something in his arms.

Something with a long neck, a board, a flat body and four long flippers...

Something everyone talked about in Loch Ness...

Tony's eyes wide opened when he saw the legendary beast.

"Dad. Have...have you found the Loch Ness Monster?" Tony exclaimed.

"Son, I am sorry I have gone for so long." Owen collapsed onto the ground.

"Take it easy, Dad Take it easy." Tony and Wilson soothed. "We are taking you home first. You will have a good rest and we will take care of everything."

Then they heard a painful inhuman cry from inside the sea cave.

"Dad, what the –"

Owen looked at the sea cave. He turned to his children, and then back to the sea cave again. Tears welled his eyes.

"Kids, I am afraid I cannot go back with you now. I have a friend inside I must save."

"Friend? Which friend? Where is Uncle Michael?" Wilson asked.

"There is no time to explain. I must go back for it. It saved my life twice."

"Who saves you? Go back in the cave? Are you kidding me? You are hurt. Dad, we will go with you."

"Stop. I have to do this myself." Owen stopped his children.

**

"But, your grandad didn't return. That was the last time we saw ever him." Uncle Tony sighed. "Before he goes, he briefly told us what I just told you. He told us how the Nessie risked its life saving him from a prehistoric alligator. He told us how Nessie brought him back to Loch Ness using its last bit of strength. And in return, he promised Nessie he would bring its offspring to the human world, away from the cruelty of prehistoric wildlife, no matter the cost."

Sam and I looked at *Coo*.

The baby plesiosaur looked back at us with its inno-cent, blank eyes.

All this time, I thought Dad has only been telling me wild stories.

I never thought it could be real.

PART 4

24

Inside the auditorium complex of the Natural History Museum, a group of cryptozoologist, government officers and museum specialist gathered in a secretive conference room, debating about the cryptid in Loch Ness.

"Dr. Parker, it has been proven times and times again that the surgeon's photo in 1934 is nothing more than an elaborate hoax!" A scientist with white beard assured. His nametag labelled Tony Ashley.

"Excuse me, doctor, are you aware there are more than one thousand sightings about the surgeon in Loch Ness? And last year was a record-breaking year of eleven sightings." Dr. Parker defended.

"Driftwood. Waves. An elephant. An otter. How many more evidence do we need to conclude the creature you are seeking simply just does not exist? It is an extraordinary delusion." Tony raised his voice.

"On 24th August 2011, Loch Ness boat captain Marcus Atkinson photographed a sonar image of a 1.5 meters unidentified object following his boat for two minutes, at a depth of 23 meters. Dr. Tony, explain to me how can it be elephant or otter?" Dr. Parker challenged.

He projected the photo on the screen.

Suddenly, the conference room is filled with a noisy crowd.

Dr. Tony paused. His eyes darted left and right, waiting for the crowd to have his attention.

"Dr. Parker, you have quite a sense of humour. Back in 2012, a scientist from the National Oceanography Center already had proven that the image is nothing more than a bloom of algae and zooplankton."

"That is not true." Dr. Parker shook his head.

"Loch Ness is only stretched about twenty-five miles long and one mile in wide. It was covered by glaciers for twenty thousand years and was only formed about ten thousand years ago. Current scientific evidence shows that plesiosaur died out sixty million years ago towards the end of Cretaceous period. Therefore, creature of the size of Nessie would have to enter the loch after the lake was fully formed, and the species would have to live much longer than scientists originally thought, do you think it is possible? Assume it is possible. But Loch Ness has limited ecological supplies. Convince me how is that sufficient to support a dinosaur of that size?" Dr. Tony continued, just like the way he schooled his son and nephew.

The crowd agreed.

"I knew it. Dr. Tony has been right. The Loch Ness Monster is nothing but a hoax."

"If the monster really exists, we could have found it by now."

The host of the museum conference came to the stage, his arthritic limbs straining against the weight of his body.

Just when he was about to announce the outcome of the debate, a young, black researcher burst into the conference room, gasping.

Dr. Tony frowned.

This kid looked familiar somehow.

Where had he seen him before?

"What is the matter, young fellow? Do you have an invitation?" The host narrowed his eyes and asked.

"I found it…" the young researcher cried breathlessly.

"What have you found?"

"The Loch Ness Monster…It's eDNA…it really exists."

25

"D r. Tony, do you have any comment about the monster's eDNA?" The crowd pursued.

Waves of bright cameras flashes blinded him.

Dr. Tony stared at Tyrone angrily.

His mind went blank and began to get off the stage.

He vowed to protect the secret of Nessie all his life.

Today, it looks like he has failed.

"So, the monster really exists?"

The crowd became sceptic once again.

"The Natural History Museum always wants the Loch Ness Monster to come to England. But, the Royal Scottish Museum believed that, if the monster existed, it should remain in Scotland." A museum officer from England spoke.

"Nonsense. If the Loch Ness Monster really exists, it should be Royal Scottish Museum's property." A representative from Royal Scottish Museum disputed.

"Stay Calm. Ladies and gentlemen, stay calm," the host silenced everyone with a judge hammer. "We mean no harm to the creature even if it exists."

"Should you ever come within range of the Loch Ness

Monster, I suggest you not be deterred by humanitarian consideration. Shoot it on the spot and send the carcass back to us in a cold, storage, and carriage forward. Even if it is not a full carcass, a flipper, a jaw or even a tooth would be very welcome." A guy in black uniform sitting at the back of the auditorium complex shouted. His shoulder badge had a Genesis logo on it.

Dr. Tony shook his head.

These people are crazy.

It is just a matter of time before people will find out about *Coo*.

There is no time.

I must take it back to where it belongs before it is too late.

26

"Hey, *Coo*. Catch!" I ordered it as I flew a boomerang away.

Coo looked at my gesture.

It slid itself forward with its flippers with full speed.

Then it raised its head.

The next thing I saw, it already caught the boomerang with its mouth.

"Wow, cool!" Sam applauded.

He threw an Atlantic salmon to it as a reward for performing the trick.

"Hey Sam, what a waste." I accursed.

"Don't worry, I don't think we will go out and fish anytime soon. Not with *Coo* around."

"I wonder how cool it is for Uncle Tony to have *Coo* as a pet all this time." I contemplated.

"Dad is very secretive. He has always been telling the world that Nessie doesn't exist. Who would have guessed he is the one who is hiding the monster himself," Sam said.

"Oh well, perhaps he doesn't want people to find out. Perhaps this is the only way that can protect *Coo*," I said.

My eyes locked on the cute plesiosaur that kept on smiling at me.

Sam and I chased it around the house.

To our surprise, *Coo* played along.

It looks like *Coo* is highly intelligent who understood us.

When we stumbled into a room, we saw a painting canvas art showing Loch Ness in the sunset.

In the middle of the loch was featuring the silhouette of a mother plesiosaur playing with its adorable baby.

It was filled with love and peace.

Coo stopped in front of the painting.

It raises its long neck and studied it thoughtfully.

Then its expression saddened and uttered a long yelp.

"Oh, poor *Coo*. It must be missing its mother." I soothed it.

"After all these years." Sam sighed.

Suddenly, a question struck me like an electric shock.

"If *Coo* was a baby plesiosaur when Uncle Tony was a kid, shouldn't it be fully grown by now?" I scratched my head.

"Yes. You are right. Why don't I think of this before?" Sam agreed. "Maybe it suffers dwarfism."

"You have to be kidding. A plesiosaur the size of a puppy after so many years?" I frowned.

"Maybe Dad purposely starved it so it cannot grow." Sam guessed thoughtfully.

"Maybe."

27

Time flies in the blink of an eye.

Another long week has passed.

Very soon, my summer school holiday will end.

I was counting down my last few days in Scotland.

This is probably the most memorable journey I ever had.

One fine morning, Uncle Tony left home for work before sunrise.

I was twisting and turning in bed.

In the middle of my sleep, I was awakened by a high pitch shriek from next room.

At first, I was thinking it was the alarm, but then I realize it was Sam.

I burst into Sam's room.

Already, I could see him sobbing. His shoulder heaved involuntarily.

"Sam, are you okay?" I asked.

"*Coo*, it…it is gone," Sam said.

He motioned his finger to the window above his desk.

I went over to have a look.

The window was wide opened.

I could see the scenic Urquhart Castle in the highlands, next to the peaceful water in Loch Ness.

The howling wind whipped my face.

"*Coo* disappeared. I still saw it yesterday night. This morning, when I tried to look for it again. It is no longer here."

"You mean…it opened the window and escaped?"

"No. I don't know. I just know it is not in the house right now." Sam sobbed, feeling upset.

We searched everywhere.

Strange. There are still no signs of *Coo*.

"If Dad finds it out we lost *Coo*, he would kill me for sure. He spent his whole life keeping this secret for Grandad and I –" Sam continued.

"Hey, don't panic. We will find it. I promise."

The two of us went outside the house.

"Loch Ness is so big. Where should we even begin?" Sam panicked.

I studied the ground thoughtfully.

It had Uncle Tony's car wheel track from the morning.

Suddenly, I have an idea.

"Sam, where is the opened window you said *Coo* escaped from?" I asked.

"Umm…it is on the other side of the house," Sam replied.

"We are in luck. This soil is wet. It is easy to hold footprints." I suggested.

"Great! By following the footprints, we can track *Coo*. Thanks, Leon, you just restore my faith," Sam said.

The two of us went over the other side of the house.

"Footprints! Yes. Footprints!"

We followed the trace *Coo* left behind.

Sam and I helped each other as we lowered ourselves down a dirty slope.

We stumbled past a thick carpet of dead leaves.

Tallgrass tickled my ankles.

A gust of wind swept dirt into my face and throat. I started to cough.

"Are you all right?" Sam asked.

I gave him an okay signal.

The wind picked up.

The leaves rustled and whispered.

I pushed passed a curtain of leaves that blocked my way with one hand.

The road curved steeply downhill.

"This way!" I swerved into another trail when I saw the footsteps suddenly did a sharp turn.

Huh? What happened?

No, wait. Besides *Coo*'s footprint, we saw something else.

Sneaker footprints.

Sam and I exchanged a worry glance.

This is no good.

But, the Loch is right up ahead. Maybe *Coo* had escaped.

We picked up our speed. Gasping.

The pinewoods on both sides of the trail became a blur of green and browns as we hurtled past.

And *Bang*!

We stumbled into someone mountainous.

He gave us a shove and knocked us onto the ground.

Our mouth dropped open when we raise our head.

It was Tyrone.

28

"Well, well, well, see who have we got here?" Tyrone grinned at us.

Jimmy soon regrouped with him from behind.

"It is the two trouble makers who almost got us into jail!" Jimmy accursed.

"I don't even know what are you talking about," I got back up on my knees.

"Oh, is that so? Brother, what shall we do to them? Should you throw them into the loch to feed the fish?" Jimmy uttered an evil laugh.

"Cut it out, we have work to do today," Tyrone scolded.

He gazed at the small footprint left by *Coo*. Then he turned to us and asked. "Hang on a second. What are the two of you doing here?"

Sam and exchanged a worried gaze.

We can't tell them we are here to find *Coo*.

But, it is kind of obvious.

"Are you here for that?" Tyrone motioned us to *Coo*'s footprints.

"No, what is that?" Sam pretended.

"Is it some kind of lamb joke? No way we will fall for

it." I added.

Tyrone didn't reply.

He came to us and whispered in our ears. "We have it. It is in our car."

Our expression changed.

"You captured *Coo*?" Sam angered. He tried to fight Tyrone but he was too weak.

With another shove, Sam fell onto the ground.

"So, the two of you know something about the Loch Ness Monster," Tyrone said.

A ringtone from Jimmy interrupted us.

"Tyrone. Dr. Parker says he will come here momentarily." Jimmy swallowed hard.

"Tell him to bring the reward." Tyrone cried repeatedly.

"Huh? But, we still haven't found the monster yet." Jimmy wondered.

"Don't worry. We are close. Besides, we have two little helpers who know about the monster," Tyrone said.

***

Tyrone and Jimmy escorted us like prisoners.

"So, tell me something about those little footprints that came from your house," Tyrone said.

"You traced them all the way to our house?" Sam was astonished.

"We did. We have tested each one of the main monster hypotheses. Three of them show a negative result and one of them might be right. We narrowed down where we collect the sample. Surprisingly, it led us right back to your holiday house." Tyrone explained.

"Truth be told, we don't believe it at first… not until we found those tiny footprints coming from your house."

Jimmy added.

"We don't know anything about that." Sam insisted.

"Very well, we shall see."

The four of us walked along the shore of Loch Ness where the footprints ended.

Several small wooden boats were left abandoned on the beach.

Under the sun, the shimmering water in Loch Ness was like a sparkling diamond.

"Let us go. There is nothing to find here," I said.

"Are you planning to stay here all day to wait for the legendary beast?" Sam joined.

"No. Of course not. You have mistaken us. I am not waiting like those people in the mountain with binoculars. I am waiting for the Loch Ness Monster to come back for you. Its name is *Coo*, am I right?" Tyrone laughed and began to bully us.

29

"Hey, let us go! You are hurting us." I cried on top of my lung.

"Scream all you like. Scream!" Jimmy laughed like a joker in the Batman movie again.

From the corner of my eyes, I saw mysterious ripple on the water, in the middle of the loch.

Oh no! *Coo*. Please don't come to us. You can't afford to expose to the world. Please don't.

A black object glided beneath the water and swam towards the shore at full speed.

SPLASH!

A long, snake-like neck exploded from the water surface.

In the blink of an eye, Tyrone was tossed sky-high, shrieking on top of his lung.

Everyone was stunned.

The creature flexed its long neck. It swung its prey left and right with agility before throwing him in the middle of the loch.

Then the creature's head turned to Jimmy.

Its reptilian eyes riveted on him.

Jimmy tried to scream, but his vocal cord was frozen.

Then we heard the sound of choppers, hovering above our head. I could barely recognize Genesis's logo on it.

"*Cooooooooo*," the creature yelped.

It gave us a sullen look before disappearing back into the loch.

It…it is *Coo*. I knew it.

It is definitely *Coo*.

What happened to it?

How come it suddenly grew so big?

"Target sighted. I repeat. Target sighted. It is swimming northeast towards a sea cave," the helicopter pilot announced over the radio.

All of a sudden, a speedboat from behind the Urquhart Castle in the highlands appeared in the water.

"Sam, that boat must be after *Coo*. Hurry. We have to go after it." I shouted.

"But we don't have anything to sail," Sam complained.

"Yes, we do. With these," I motioned to the abandoned boats on the beach.

We pushed the nearest wooden boat into the water with all our strength.

Then we grabbed a paddle each and raced after the speedboat.

The engine of the speedboat rumbled.

"It is too fast, we will never be able to catch up with it," I grumbled.

"Don't worry, I know where *Coo* is heading," Sam said, gasping as he paddled.

"Where?"

"It is heading towards the sea cave."

Uncle Tony's words came back to my mind.

Suddenly, Sam began to turn back.

"Huh? Sam, what are you doing?" I asked.

"We will never be able to catch up with the speedboat like this. But, I know a better way." Sam smiled.

30

I followed Sam back to the holiday house.

We went back to the dusty, old basement filled with abandoned furniture.

We opened the trap door and lowered ourselves down the short ladder into Uncle Tony's lab.

We walked past the huge table with computers and apparatus.

The pink solution in the test tube with Genesis's logo captured my eyes once again.

"Leon, why do you stop?" Sam asked at the doorway to the subterranean lake.

"Sam, do you feel something strange?" I asked.

"The world is strange ever since we discovered the Loch Ness Monster." Sam agreed.

"No. I mean this logo. I mean Genesis. We saw it on the chopper too." I recall.

"Yes. You are right." Sam began to feel suspicious. "It doesn't make any sense. Why is Genesis's logo appearing in Dad's secret lab?"

I searched the logo on the Internet.

Dozens of news popped up about its pioneering genetic breakthroughs around the world.

It even had a theme park titled "Genetic Park".

"I thought Uncle Tony is working for the museum only." I raise my eyebrows.

Just as we were about to head to the subterranean lake, one of the lockers at the far end of the lab drew our attention.

BANG BANG BANG

It was the same sound we hear before.

Someone is banging from inside the locker.

BANG BANG BANG

"Who...who is that?" Sam and I startled.

The banging sound continued.

This time it is even more vicious.

"Sam, don't open it. You don't know what is inside," I pulled him back.

"No. Wait. I have to see who it is. I can't accept strange noise in my house," Sam insisted.

"All right, but be careful."

Step by step, we moved towards the locker.

"Counting. One. Two. Three."

We took a deep breath and opened the locker.

To our surprise, we found Uncle Tony and Aunty Belly! Their hands and feet were tied.

Their mouth gagged by a wide strip of white tape.

"Mom? Dad?" Sam was surprised.

I was absolutely stunned.

"*Mmmmmmmm*," Uncle Tony and Aunty Belly stared at us with pleading eyes.

They struggled to speak through the gag.

"Mom, I thought you are on a vacation in Africa, chased by animals. Dad, I thought you are working in the museum." Sam startled.

We pull the tape off our aunty and uncle's mouth and untied them.

"Leon, how come you are here?" Uncle Tony asked breathlessly.

"Uncle Tony, you picked me up at the airport, don't you remember?" I asked, my voice came out startled.

"Can someone tell me what is going on?" Sam asked. His expression worried.

Uncle Tony and Aunty Belly exchanged a worried gaze with each other.

Reluctantly, they began to speak.

31

"*C oo*, don't leave me, please. I promise father to take good care of you. I will bring you back to Nessie. I will bring you back to your mother. Hang in there." Tony sobbed, his arms wrapped around the prehistoric pet.

The happy moment it had with him since childhood flashback in his mind.

The prehistoric creature looked at Tony in its weary eyes, gasping for air.

It is too late.

Tony's eyes locked on *Coo*.

He brushed its head with his hand.

"It is all my fault. I am too selfish. I shouldn't keep you with me all these years. You have grown too big. You should have gone back home. The human world is not suitable for you. Pollution. Overfishing. Every day, you need to hide." Tony sobbed.

Betty came over. She kneeled down next to *Coo*.

"Tony, don't lose faith. Perhaps we should send it to the Veterinary physician. Perhaps they might have something that can save it." Betty suggested.

"Betty, I can't. You know what will happen if I expose

Coo to the world, don't you?" Tony rejected.

"I do," Betty says is a low voice. "But – "

Tony stopped her.

"I know there are other ways. I know there must be other ways." Tony murmured to himself.

He took out a newspaper that titled: The scientific world was in an uproar yesterday after Scottish researchers broke one of Mother Nature's strongest taboos by cloning a mammal – a staggering breakthrough that opens the door to copying human beings.

"Betty, trust me. I know there are other ways."

***

"Dad, what I saw wasn't the real child of Nessie, isn't it? The real child of Nessie was already dead. What we saw was a clone, isn't it?" Sam asked.

Uncle Tony nodded.

"Soon, Betty and I began to work for Genesis. In the beginning, I specialize in cloning human embryos for the purpose to extract stem cells. Because of my success rate, soon, I got promoted into one of the chief geneticists. I never forget my ultimate goal is to revive *Coo*, I tricked Genesis into believing I will accelerate the growth of clones. I got funding from them to buy this place and renovate it as a disguise for my personal underground research facility. Then things began to turn diplomatic." Uncle Tony revealed.

"Loch Ness is a sensitive area. A lot of Genesis scientists envy Tony. A lot of them are trying to make the Loch Ness legend a reality, but with little success. They fear that Tony is a threat to them, that is why they join forces together to create a cloned Tony - one that acts as their puppet." Aunty Betty explained.

"That is insane. Cloning human is illegal!" Sam accursed.

"I can't distinguish between the real Uncle Tony and the clone," I said.

"The cloned Uncle Tony is dangerous. He even has Tony's memory." Aunty Betty added.

"Uncle Tony, we got to be quick. Right now, *Coo* is on the loose. It has grown so big. It even attacked Tyrone. And it is escaping to the sea cave northeast of Loch Ness."

"Genesis is after it. I bet it is on the news headline by now," Sam said.

"Then we have to hurry." Uncle Tony said. "We have to make sure *Coo* doesn't get captured by Genesis."

He motioned us to the sturdy door to the subterranean lake.

"This way."

32

Once again, we are back in the subterranean lake.

"Oh, it stinks." Sam complained, and cupped his hands around his nose and mouth "Dad, I can't believe how you can work next door."

"It stinks to you. But, *Coo* loves it. It resembles its home." Uncle Tony said.

He hopped inside the yellow boat anchored to a hook by a rope, next to a ram.

Aunty Betty, Sam and I followed shortly after and began to sail.

"Uncle Tony, are you sure *Coo* will come back here?" I asked.

"It has to. This is its home." Uncle Tony answered.

"But, it is not big enough for it anymore.' I challenged.

"You have no idea where this leads to, don't you?" Aunty Betty asked.

"It is connected back to the Loch Ness, right?" I guessed.

Uncle Tony and Aunty Betty looked at each other.

Then they began to laugh.

"Huh? What is so funny?"

"This subterranean lake does not only lead back to Loch Ness. It branched out to an uncharted landmass." Uncle Tony revealed.

He paddled pass uneven stone column and stalactites, into a wide opening, and continued to sail north.

The bright circles from our torches danced on the stalactites.

The rhythmical water dripping sound was crystal clear.

Soon, we heard the sound of a waterfall.

From a distance, the waterfall looked like a silent white stream.

"Uncle Tony, how do you know the way?"

"I have been venturing in here with your aunty for a very long time. I insisted that your Grandad is some-where on the other side so we explored it bit by bit."

"I remember we got lost a few times. But, luckily, every time we got lost, we progressed further."

The sound of the waterfall grew louder.

The light from my torch revealed white water cascaded down a series of rocky outcrops.

The water tinkled.

Louder and louder.

I could no longer hear Uncle Tony over the deafening roar of the water.

Torrents of water travelled in its path.

Closer and closer, we were drawn.

Soon, I could feel frenzied drops of water paddled against my face.

The breeze of the water was freezing cold.

"Uncle Tony? Are you going to get us wet?" I startled.

33

Before I realize, our wooden boat was propelled forward by a powerful water current.

I choked a mouthful of water when we passed the white curtain of water.

My whole body was wet.

"Hold on tight!" Uncle Tony screamed.

Without warning, our boat started sliding.

"*Wowwwwwwwwwwww.*"

The slide was curved and curved.

I was swirling down in complete darkness.

It is like I am in some kind of roller coaster ride.

Faster and faster.

I tried to look at Uncle Tony and Aunty Betty.

But it was too dark, and I was moving too fast.

Bump!

Our boat hit a boulder and everyone was pushed forward.

Bump!

"*Ouch!*"

We hit another boulder and I collided into Sam.

Finally, the curve ended abruptly.

And we were in some kind of ancient sea cave.

*****

"Alpha Team, report." Dr. Parker called over the radio repeatedly.

But, all he could hear is nothing but static.

Next to him was his opposition, Dr. Tony, who disbelief the existence of the Loch Ness Monster the whole time.

Ever since the helicopter pilot announced he had sighted the asset in the Loch Ness shore, Genesis gave orders to their securities team nearby to investigate. That is why they were dragged along.

Right now, they are outside a sea cave northeast of Loch Ness.

It loomed over them like the mouth of an almighty worm with impenetrable blackness.

The interior of the cavern looked deep.

The stonewall was jagged and uneven.

From outside, the cavern could worm at least miles into an unknown domain. The wall above arched another hundred feet up to some giant stalactites.

"Dr. Tony, shall we go in? Loch Ness is your domain." Dr. Parker asked.

"Certainly." Dr. Tony forced a smile.

He motioned the remaining two security speedboats to follow them.

"Dr. Tony, are you sure about this?" Their sailor asked, swallowing hard. "If they come with us too, we will have no more backup."

"Are you questioning my authority?" Dr. Tony asked sharply and flashed his Genesis badge. "We are the back up of Alpha Team."

"Follow the orders, solider." Dr. Parker added.

The three security boats sailed slowly inside the cave.

Chilling blackness engulfed them.

Even they turned on the headlights, there is no way of telling how deep the cave was.

Ahead was the sound of water dripping into the water.

It was crystal clear.

Dr. Parker illuminated the water with his torch.

Apparently, the turquoise water in loch Ness was replaced by murky and thick green pea soup.

It smelt disguising.

"Dr. Tony, which way shall we go?" The sailor asked.

Ahead of them was a junction that branched out into the sea cavern.

"Left, we take left." Dr. Tony replied as if he knows the way.

"Dr. Tony, have you been here before?" Dr. Parker asked suspiciously.

"No. Why would I come to this type of place?" Dr. Tony replied.

"Nothing. It is just that I am impressed with you. It looks like you already know the way," Dr. Parker faked a smile.

The three security boats sailed deeper and deeper.

Above their head was a forest of stalactites and stalagmites of irregular shapes.

The place looked menace and unexplored.

The ambient was frigid.

The temperature dropped like a rock the deeper they sail.

It had been another half an hour already.

Their radio was still unresponsive.

Somehow, they felt like they were isolated from the outside world.

Then they heard something.

It was the sound of a waterfall.

So, there is a waterfall inside nowhere in a sea cave. How intriguing.

"Dr. Tony, it is dead end." The sailor reported.

"Sail pass the waterfall." Dr. Tony commanded.

"Doctor, this is suicide. It could just be rocks." The sailor refused.

"If it is a dead-end, the water stagnant. Have a good look at the water current leading to the waterfall, it is strong." Dr. Tony disagreed.

"Dr. Tony is right. Forward, and prepare to get wet," Dr. Parker ordered.

And the three security boats disappeared behind the peculiar waterfall.

34

Our flashlight beamed found and tracked tunnels that branched off from the main junction.

"This part of the cave is unusually roomy," I whispered.

"Keep your eyes open. It is an uncharted territory," Uncle Tony said.

He directed his light on the wall and ceiling.

Then something caught the corner of our eyes.

"Stop, sail back a little bit. This is unusual." Aunty Belly asked.

"What is it, darling?"

Our eyes followed Aunty Belly's circle light.

We scrutinized the surface of the wall.

"Oh my god." Sam swallowed hard.

The wall was embedded with thousands of bones. Bones. Fossils. Everywhere. Fragments of something even Uncle Tony couldn't identify.

"I thought we are only after *Coo*." I swallowed hard.

"Perhaps we should collect these bones and see if there are any recoverable DNA," Uncle Tony said.

Just when he was about to do so, we saw the light from another branched tunnel in the main sea cavern.

"It might be Genesis's security," Uncle Tony whispered. "Switch off the light now!"

The sound of the noisy motor sang in our ears.

Louder and louder.

It looks like they are heading in our direction.

Circles of beam danced randomly on the wall and the ceiling.

Occasionally, it just missed me and landed on the bones embedded on the high wall.

My heart was beating quickly.

What if they spot us? Will they throw us into the water and left us here? No one would have known we come to this uncharted territory.

Dozens of questions raised in my mind.

Suddenly, we heard something disturbed the water.

And the beam of light was drawn away.

SPLASHES

I vaguely saw greenish scaly skin slithered through the waves like a snake.

Is that *Coo*? I couldn't tell.

"Captain. Target sighted." One of Genesis's security guards in black uniform reported. His voice was hoarse, filled with static.

"Dead or alive, it is coming with us." The captain ordered.

"Affirmative." The security guard made an offensive stance and aimed at the ripples.

Oh nooooo. They are going to kill *Coo*.

Sam and I exchanged a worry glance.

Just before we decided to throw something in the water to distract the guard, something bumped against the underside of Genesis's speedboat.

"What the?" The security guard staggered.

"Look! There is another one!" Sam pointed to a column of reptilian skin that broke the surface.

"No. There are more." Uncle Tony corrected.

My mouth dropped open in surprise when I saw the speedboats were surrounded by a school of unknown aquatic creatures from all sides.

Three. Four. Five. No.

Water disturbance can be seen everywhere.

There were more of them coming from all sides!

35

"Oh, my god!" The guard shrieked as a behemoth alligator jaw broke the surface with monstrous teeth.

When it disappeared again, the water turned crimson.

Its malevolent, amber eyes locked on the remaining guards on the deck.

I don't need to know what the rest of its body looks like.

For me, the head we saw was enough.

"GO GO GO!" Aunty Belly urged.

We helped Uncle Tony to paddle as fast as we could with all our strength.

Behind us was a churning mess of whipping tail and snapping teeth.

The shooting sound, scream and inhuman shriek filled the air.

Now, I know why Nessie rather left its baby to the human world.

I gazed at Uncle Tony with the same blank look like me.

I finally know why.

***

"Dr. Tony, the Alpha team is in trouble."

Dr. Parker and his team listened as the last firing died down.

Everything was silent again.

"Doctor?" The sailor asked again.

"This is fascinating." Dr. Tony spoke.

"Excuse me?" The sailor frowned.

The doctor didn't reply.

He pointed to a wounded beast that just partly lifted its head above the water for air.

The creature has a long, slender neck, and reptilian skin.

When it saw the beam of the torch, it submerged again.

"It is a rewarding trip. Follow the water disturbance." Dr. Tony urged.

"But, doctor, what about the alpha team –" The sailor asked again, but was interrupted by Dr. Tony.

"Solider, our mission is to capture Nessie, not to save Alpha," Dr. Tony said coldly.

Reluctantly, the sailor obeyed.

They ventured to pass a narrow tunnel that branched into a large opening.

Then they saw a curved wall filled with cave bones and fossils.

"Are these some kind of dinosaurs' bones?"

Some guards worried when they saw large bones hanging loosely on the curved cave wall.

"No. It belongs to one only." Dr. Tony studied the wall carefully.

Their heart almost skipped a beat when they realize the fossil stretched at least forty feet long!

Whatever that animal was, it is a behemoth.

They continued to follow the sluggish water disturbance.

Then they saw a spot of light that at the far end of the tunnel.

At first, they thought it was a flashlight.

But, then, the light grows brighter and brighter...

"I think we have finally reached the exit of the sea cave."

36

The wounded sea serpent used its last bit of strength and collapsed outside the sea cave.

Gasping for its last breath.

It did its best to fend off the other sea creatures from attacking Uncle Tony – the boy who raises it in the human world.

They shouldn't have followed it.

But, it knows why they followed.

They want to know it is safe.

The poor creature pushed itself forward with its weak flippers.

It was bathed in the warmth of the sun.

Pieces of scattered memories came back to its mind.

This place is its birthplace. Or is it?

It looks familiar.

But, at the same time, it looks foreign.

Why is that?

The creature yelped.

The blurred image of its mother came to its mind.

It remembers the beautiful Loch Ness in the sunset.

In the middle of the loch was featuring the silhouette

of a mother plesiosaur playing with its adorable baby.

Coo. Coo.

It heard footsteps from behind.

A long shadow cast over it and blocked the sun.

Dr. Parker and the Genesis security guards couldn't believe their eyes.

It…it is the legendary Loch Ness Monster.

"So, the legend is true. Loch Ness Monster really exists," Dr. Parker laughed.

"You are a naughty one," Dr. Tony smiled at the creature.

He fired a net gun at the wretched creature.

Coo tried to escape but its body was entangled.

It raised its long neck and saw Tony – the boy who raise it and protect it all its life.

Astonished. Betrayed. Sorrow.

It just doesn't understand why Tony has to change sides.

Perhaps it is because it grew so big all of a sudden.

Perhaps it is because it attacked people in Loch Ness.

But, it doesn't matter anymore.

"Bring it back alive," Dr. Tony ordered his troops.

"Wait!"

A voice from nowhere interrupted them.

When Dr. Parker turned raised his head, he saw another Dr. Tony on top of a rocky ledge.

Confused.

He backed off from Dr. Tony next to him immediately.

"What is going on?" Dr. Parker asked.

"It looks like Genesis made a copy of me," The clone pointed to the real Uncle Tony from the ledge. "Let my family go."

"No. You are the actual clone!" Uncle Tony accursed.

"Guards, shoot the clone. Save my family." The clone ordered.

But, the guards ignored him.

"What are you waiting for? Shoot the clone," The clone roared.

"Dr. Tony, our mission is to capture Nessie, not to shoot clones," the securities declined.

"Genesis created you because I do not want to cooperate with them and tell them the secret behind Loch Ness." Uncle Tony revealed.

"Lair. I am the real one." The clone ignored him.

"Uncle Tony, it looks like he doesn't believe he is a fake," I whispered.

"Dr. Parker, you want to proof the Loch Ness Monster exists. And now, you saw it. It is a clone. I hope by now, you realize how dangerous it is to bring prehistoric creatures back to life in the human world. It is Genesis's game plan. The Alpha team had been annihilated. I saw it with my own eyes." Uncle Tony warned.

Dr. Parker was undecided.

He looked at the poor creature, and then Dr. Tony beside him.

"These dinosaurs, they cannot adapt to our world. I have tried my entire life. *Coo*, Nessie's son died because of this. Dinosaur and human simply cannot coexist. My whole life, I want to bring it back. I have even recreated an entire environment just for it. I have found a solution to suppress and accelerate growth. I think I can cheat nature. But, I was wrong."

"Enough talk!" The clone roared.

He grabbed a pistol from one of the security guards.

Just when he began to fire, *Coo* torn the nest with its last bit of strength. It raced to knock the clone over.

BANG!

Everything happened too quickly.

The next thing we saw, *Coo* and the clone collapsed onto the ground.

37

"Huh? Pink blood? How?" The clone watched in horror as pink blood dripped from his wound.

He looked at *Coo*, which bleeds the same blood as him.

Coo Coo

An inhuman yelp drew everyone to the horizontal.

With a splash, another long snake-like neck rose above the turquoise water.

Its eyes glowered down at him.

"Nessie!" Uncle Tony cried excitedly.

"Insufferable beast!" The clone tried to put a bullet in Nessie's head, but it was too quick.

It yanked down its head, swooped the clone up its mouth, and snapped.

Dr. Parker opened his mouth, but no sound came out.

The remaining Genesis securities looked at the almighty creature and collapsed to their feet.

"Leave and never return." Nessie roared angrily.

Sam, Aunty Betty, Uncle Tony and I raced down the slope to greet Nessie and *Coo*. I am surprised Nessie can actually talk in English.

"Nessie, you live?" Tony's eyes were filled with a mixture of emotions.

Nessie nodded.

It lowered its head to the dying *Coo*.

"I am sorry, Nessie,"

"No. It is not your fault. The prehistoric world is cruel. Every day, I worry about *Coo*. Every day, I worry that one day, when I return back to the sea cave, *Coo* is no longer there. On a rare occasion, I saved your father, who became good friends with me. I begged your father to bring *Coo* to the human world, thinking it might be a safer place." Nessie spoke. "But, I was wrong."

"I tried to bring *Coo* back, but I was too late…" Uncle Tony said softly.

Nessie lowered its head and looked at its cloned son.

Deep inside, it knew he is not the real *Coo*.

It studied him. It wanted to believe he is its real son.

But, the truth is that he is not.

Coo looked at Nessie.

It always wishes one day it could see its mother.

That day had come.

Its wish has finally come true. It has no regret.

Then its eyes began to close.

The dying scene of the cloned *Coo* was like a dagger through Nessie's heart.

Its lips quivered.

It titled its long neck high above the sky and yelped.

The silhouette of Nessie moaned behind the pink and orange sky.

"Uncle Tony, is there another way to save *Coo*?" I urged.

"I could have saved it if we are inside the lab. Now, I am afraid I can do nothing."

"What is missing?" Sam asked.

"I need the pink solution. I need the pink solution that can stimulate cell growth." Uncle Tony sighed.

"Do you mean this?" I reached out for my pocket and took out a corked test tube filled with the pink solution.

The magical pink solution.

38

Do you believe in the Loch Ness Monster?

Maybe you do. Maybe you don't.

No matter what you believe in, one thing I do know is this urban legend will continue to live on.

Soon after Nessie escorted us back home that day, we made a promise to her not to disclose the secret of Loch Ness.

This uncharted landmass is just too dangerous to visit.

"*Coo*, we are going to miss you," Sam and I brushed our hands-on *Coo*'s head.

"Meeeeee you," *Coo* tried to mimic but it came out rather cute.

Everyone laughed.

For me, I don't care whether *Coo* is a clone.

I don't care whether its blood is pink or red.

I don't care whether it is born naturally or from a test tube.

After all, what happens to me is that it is alive.

All living things deserve the right to be respected.

Don't you think so?

"Thank you for trying to bring *Coo* back." Nessie

thanked. "Thank you for trying to protect my child. But, I think I will not visit Loch Ness for a very long time."

"Genesis will not give up so easily." Uncle Tony assured. "But, I can assure that what happened in Loch Ness stays in Loch Ness."

***

"Leon, shall we continue where we left off?" Dad teased.

"Dad, didn't Mom ask you not to tell me wild stories at night?" I raise my eyebrows.

"Well, of course I know I shouldn't. But, don't you want to know what Grandad saw that night?" Dad tried to convince me.

"He saw Nessie," I said. "And, they became good friends."

"Huh? How do you know?" Dad was shocked.

"Dad, I think I know a lot more than you. Maybe it is time for me to tell you bedtime stories instead." I teased back.

"Try me." Dad gave me a broad smile.

That night, after I came home, I had an impulse.

I want to write about the journey.

I want to record down everything I been through in Loch Ness.

I kept thinking about Nessie and Grandad.

After that, I thought about *Coo*.

Perhaps fate brought us together.

I sat in front of a blank page, trying to find the right words for the title of my story.

Then a title struck my head.

My Loch Ness Journey.

TERRORLANDS

READER BEAWARE : YOU MAY BE IN FOR A SCARE

MARCO CHU KWAN CHING

About the Author

Marco Chu Kwan Ching's books are read all over the world. Apart from the Terrorlands Series, Marco Chu Kwan Ching is also the author of two books, *Corruption of Real Money* and *Legacy of Debt*.

You can learn more about his work at

www.terrorlands.com

www.corruptionofrealmoney.com

When he is not writing, he loves working on Fiverr. He has thousands of happy customers around the world.

https://www.fiverr.com/mckcvision

Marco Chu Kwan Ching lives in Australia with his wife, Carrie.

Thank you for Reading!

If you love my work, please feel free to leave a positive feedback on Amazon and Goodreads.

My contact:
https://www.facebook.com/marco.chu.10
https://www.goodreads.com/author/show/15944678.Marco_Chu_Kwan_Ching

Terrorlands Facebook Page
https://www.facebook.com/terrorlands/

Terrorlands Twitter Page
https://twitter.com/terrorlands

Goodreads Page
https://www.goodreads.com/book/show/47950091-my-loch-ness-journey

Terrorlands Website
http://www.terrorlands.com